PILLION FOR A
POLICE OFFICER

By Fleur Blüm

Fleur Blüm is a Melbourne-based writer, performer and musician.

Her blog can be found at https://fleurblum.com/blog

Also by Fleur Blüm
Sophie's Path: A choose your own romance adventure
Discovering the Franklins
My Mother's Secret
The Sins of the Father: a Barrett Women novel
The Mother's Fault: a Barrett Women novel
Singular Focus
Singular Purpose
Morgana, My Queen

Poetry Collections:
My Body. No Apology
Consider the Watchmaker
Smells Like Teen Angst

First edition 2025

Copyright © 2024 Fleur Blüm
ISBN: 978-0-6483654-8-8

Editor: Sarah Lamb
Cover Design: Get Covers

Published by Fleur Blüm, Melbourne, Australia

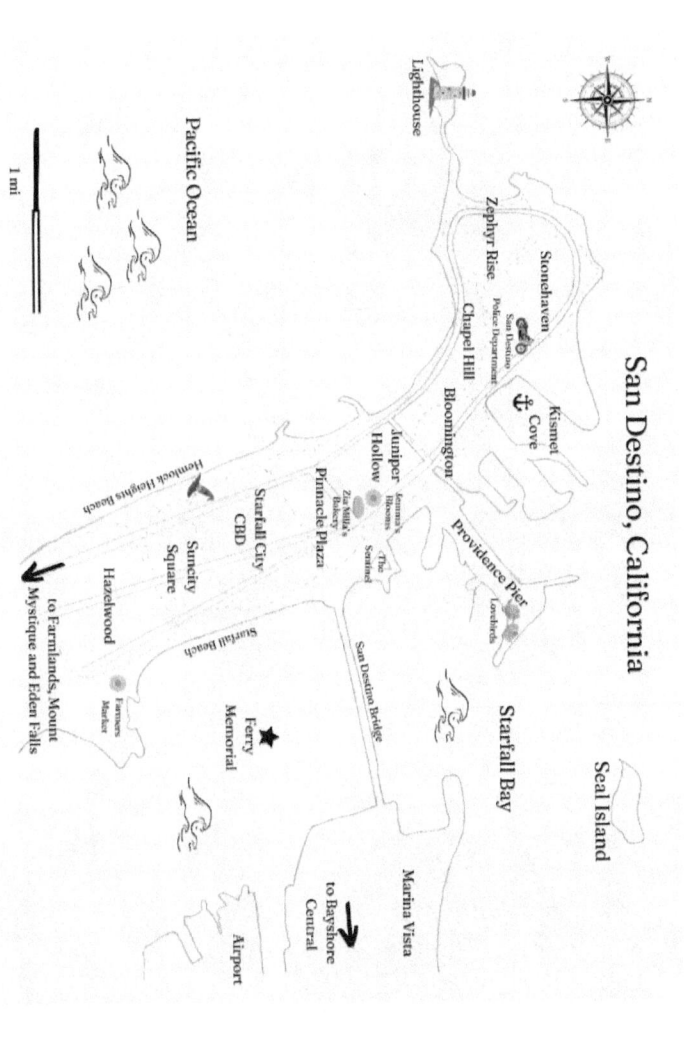

San Destino, California

Seal Island

Pacific Ocean

1 mi

Lighthouse

Zephyr Rise

Stonehaven

Chapel Hill

Bloomington

Kismet Cove

San Destino Police Department

Juniper Hollow

Memma's Blooms

The Sentinel

Zia Mia's Bakery

Providence Pier

Lovebirds

Starfall City CBD

Pinnacle Plaza

Hemlock Heights Beach

Suncity Square

Hazelwood

Starfall Beach

Farmers Market

Ferry Memorial

San Destino Bridge

Starfall Bay

Marina Vista

to Bayshore Central

Airport

to Farmlands, Mount Mystique and Eden Falls

Chapter 1

Petra Gillies sat in an uncomfortable molded plastic chair next to a bed. The bed was very nicely made up, you could almost forget it was a hospital bed. The woman in it was breathing shallowly, paper-thin eyelids restless as she dozed. Margaret's hand was frail and bony in Petra's. The old lady was dying, and it was Petra's job, her privilege, to help her pass over.

Margaret didn't have any children. Her siblings and friends had already gone over to the other side, so when she asked Petra to be her companion, her death doula, the younger woman happily agreed. It wasn't her usual job, Petra worked as a yoga instructor in a bustling local studio, but people had a way of knowing about her special talents, the ones she didn't talk about.

There were a few more minutes until it was Margaret's time. Petra felt it in her core, she was near, but not quite there.

She had first noticed she wasn't like other people when she knew her mother was hiding an illness. It was as though there was a big angry red circle over her abdomen for weeks until Mary admitted she had a stomach ulcer that needed treatment.

Petra was only ten at the time, but after that she kept an eye out for unusual things she noticed that others didn't. When her grandmother died, Petra was in high school, and she could see her time running out clearly. It wasn't exactly seeing, more like she just knew. When her grandmother's time was nearly up, Petra took her hand, and whispered in her ear:

"It's okay, Nanna. There's nothing to fear on the other side, it's just like falling asleep." She had looked into her grandmother's pale blue eyes and watched the fear slip away as her last breath left her body. For a few moments afterwards, it was as though time was suspended, then a sudden silence, like someone had turned off a buzzing light.

Petra thought it must have been the sound of her grandmother's soul going out of the world. Now, every time she sat with someone in their final moments, she whispered reassuring words, different each time, as though the right words for the person were suddenly in her mouth without her thinking about it, followed by that silence after their soul had gone.

She was here with Margaret because the staff in the hospice knew she was good with the dying. They wouldn't have been able to tell anyone how they knew, or what Petra did. Most people in San Destino learned not to ask too many questions when strange things happened, even if they didn't have special talents of their own.

Margaret would go in her sleep. It was clear now the energy in her body was folding itself up, pulling up the stakes, turning off the lights, ready to go for the last time. Petra started to hum, a tune that didn't have a name, maybe Margaret's favorite song from when she was young, or maybe the song on the radio when her lover had kissed her back in the sixties. Strange things often happened when Petra did her death watch.

Fifteen minutes later, time had gone back to its normal pace and a special silence had fallen over the room. Petra stood up, placed Margaret's hand back on her chest, and kissed her cheek.

"Goodbye, my love." They weren't her words, but they seemed to fit.

When she passed the nurses' station, on her way out, one of the staff looked up.

"Is she gone?"

"Yes, all finished."

"I hope it was easy. She'd had a rough time of it these last few weeks."

"Oh yes, she just slipped away to sail across the still waters into Death's waiting arms. Nothing to it." Petra blinked. "I didn't know I was going to say that." She laughed.

"Very poetic. Margaret loved poetry," the nurse said.

"It must have been for her then." Petra smiled and walked to the elevators. The after effects of a death lingered for different periods of time. Maybe it had something to do with the strength of a soul, or how much influence they had on their surroundings, she didn't know. Petra always stayed alone until she returned to her usual bubbly self after her death duties. Other people tended not to understand why she acted out of character.

***

"Central to four-Mary-five," a voice crackled over Riley Holmes's radio.

"Four-Mary-five, go ahead," she replied.

"There's an accident up on the Destiny Bridge, all lanes blocked. We need you to get out there and help with directing traffic."

"Copy, in route." Riley put the mic back onto its cradle and turned over the engine of her police issue motorcycle.

It's far too early for this. Sergeant Riley Holmes had hoped for a quiet day watching traffic after being up half the previous night with her mother, Georgina. Georgina had developed a worrying cough in addition to her long list of chronic ailments and needed her eldest daughter to help with her care.

San Destino Bridge, or Destiny Bridge as the locals called it, was the main connecting arterial from San Destino to the mainland, and a blockage on it would create havoc. Especially if the inbound and outbound lanes were both affected.

Riley saw the obstruction coming along Bridge Road past the towering Sentinel building. Vehicles had already backed up, almost to the gateway onto the mainland, and onto the island behind her, by the time she arrived. Being on her bike had its benefits; she could work her way to the front and assist.

Pillion for a Police Officer

Two lanes in each direction, the single span bridge had been built in the late forties to replace the ferry when it sank. A large white postal van was completely blocking the outbound lanes. It had crushed the back end of a bright florist's van, which now cut off the inbound lanes. Besides the two vans, there was debris everywhere—shattered glass, letters, flowers, and parcels spilled all over the road.

Behind the collision on her side, three cars that hadn't been able to get out of the way of whatever had happened and had rear-ended one another adding to the general confusion on the bridge. On the mainland side, inbound to San Destino, the drivers seemed to have stopped in time for the most part.

Riley was the first officer on scene. Over the wind, more sirens sounded behind her—probably an ambulance trying to get through. She would need to keep the inbound side of the road clear for emergency service vehicles, though cars on both sides of the bridge had already started to turn around and drive back the way they had come.

"Four-Mary-Five to Central."

"Come in Four-Mary-Five," a voice replied.

"We're gonna need a roadblock established at the entrance to Destiny Bridge on both sides. Postal van has crashed, all four lanes are completely impassable. Unclear if there are serious injuries as yet." Riley scanned the vehicles she could see on the island side, looking into the windows of the three cars that had piled up.

Strong, cold winds blew across Starfall Bay, swirling handfuls of letters and flowers off the bridge and into the water. The hairs on the back of her neck and arms stood up, an ominous feeling gripping her body, but Riley pulled her attention back to the task at hand—triaging the injuries while the paramedics were making their way to her position. She pulled out her first aid kit.

The back car, the first Riley came to, was a ridiculous pink Volvo. Inside, a woman in her forties and a teen girl, both with bleached blonde hair, probably mother and daughter, sat in what appeared to be shock. Riley peered into the driver's side window and pulled on her blue disposable gloves.

"Are you okay in there?" She attempted to open the door.

"I think so. Just a little shook up." The female driver had some cuts on her face that were bleeding heavily but didn't seem too serious.

"Don't try to move. Best to stay still in case you have an injury you're not aware of," Riley said, handing the woman a square gauze pad. "Hold that on your cheek. Paramedics are on their way, okay?"

"Sure, Officer," the woman said, nodding her head a little, then wincing as she pushed the gauze into one of the larger cuts. Riley turned to check the progress of the ambulance, and now a fire truck also approached the entrance of the bridge. Both blaring sirens, though the roadblock hadn't been set up yet; drivers were still trying to turn onto the bridge.

In the second car, a two-door blue Toyota hatchback, Riley found a man in his late sixties looking very pale and unmoving.

"Sir, can you hear me?" She tried the door. This time it didn't pull open as the woman's car had. Had he locked the door for safety, or was it the result of the collision?

She knocked on the window and called out again, but the man remained still, his head at a strange angle, his eyes closed, though his chest moving up and down as he breathed. She tried the door one more time, then looked into the car that had collided with the postal van.

Check it, then come back and try to open this guy's door. Riley went to the front car, a green Suburban, its nose crumbled into the side of the postal van, windshield smashed. When she tried the door, it opened easily. Inside, a wealthy looking man in his forties, his shirt and tie streaked with blood, sat stunned.

"Sir, are you okay?"

He flickered his eyes to her. "I think so. No need to worry about me, Sergeant."

Riley glanced around the cabin. "Are you on the job, sir?"

He laughed, then winced. "Retired. Check the other fellow. He's not moving. I'm alright here till paramedics arrive."

The postal van was empty. Marge, the driver, sat on the curb while a civilian attended to her.

Riley returned to the blue hatchback. The old man inside hadn't moved. She didn't carry a slim jim in her tool kit, the bike had limited space, and she regretted not

13

having one today. Riley went around to the other side of the hatchback, back past the mother and daughter, who looked pale, but stable.

The passenger side of the hatchback was a little less banged up than the driver's side door. Riley tried the door again, and this time it pulled open with a squeak. Just as she was about to get into the car, the ambulance finally made it to their position.

"First and last cars seem to be minor injuries, and fairly stable. This guy I'm worried about," she yelled to the two paramedics who went straight into action. "I'll see if I can get the door open from inside." She ducked her head into the car, checking for dangerous objects before leaning over toward the driver. "Sir? Are you with us?"

Riley prodded his arm gently, but he didn't respond. His breathing was shallow and labored.

"I'm going to try to open the door to let the paramedics in," she said, in case he could hear her. "No need to worry. We'll have you sorted out shortly."

The door was unlocked, and when she pulled the handle, nothing happened. Riley crawled a little further inside and tried again, this time with a firm shove for good measure, but it was stuck. The one thing she liked about older style cars in these situations was the hand crank windows. She started to turn the handle to give the paramedics room.

"Door's stuck," she said, though it was obvious.

"I'll come 'round," the shorter of the paramedics said, then scooted over the hood of the car behind on his butt. "If you don't mind, Officer…"

Riley backed out of the car to allow access. "Holmes. Riley Holmes," she replied.

"Thanks, Riley. We've got it from here."

Riley turned away from the scene, allowing the medicos to do their jobs. "Four-Mary-five to central," she said over the radio.

"Central, go ahead four-Mary-five."

"Paramedics in place on this side. Have we got that roadblock up yet?"

"Yes, roadblock is in place. We have units coming to you to help direct traffic away from the collision site."

"Copy." Riley wanted to go to the other side of the crash, but the road was unsafe to do so, even on foot. She moved to get a better vantage point. An ambulance had arrived on the far side as well as police vehicles. It seemed the mainland side had been able to send people more efficiently. She was still waiting for another unit to back her up.

Those caught behind the line of cars in the crash continued to try and turn around.

I need to do something. The first uninjured car in the line had rolled down their driver's side window and the woman leaned her head out as though to catch Riley's attention.

"Are you hurt, ma'am?" Riley jogged toward the car.

"No, we're not hurt. I can see the cars behind turning around. Are we okay to go?"

"Did you see what happened?"

"No, not really," the woman replied. "One minute we were driving along no worries, and the next there was a flash of something over the road, a screech of tires, and the postal van started swerving all over the road. Then I think it must have hit the wall on the other side, and at some point it rolled over. It was hard to see."

Riley pulled out her small notepad and took down what the woman said. "Okay, then what happened?"

"The cars in front couldn't stop in time, although I braked as soon as the van started swerving."

"You said a flash of something. What do you mean by that?"

"An animal on the road, I think. Sort of tan and brown spots, maybe a dog, I didn't really see."

"Strange, I'll make a note. Can I get your name and details for the report? We may need to interview you more thoroughly at a later time."

"Yes, of course." The woman gave Riley her details.

"Here's my business card. It's got my name— Sergeant Riley Holmes. If you think of anything else, please get in touch with me directly, or call the San Destino Police Department and they'll be able to help you. You can turn around and head back to the island, slowly."

Riley waved the car behind forward and repeated the same question. The driver of that car had seen even less. Even so, she got his details, handed him her card, and sent him away.

The third car was a familiar late model silver Porsche 911. The top was down, and the driver nodded to her, removing his aviator sunglasses as he approached.

"Mike," Riley said, nodding acknowledgment to her friend Petra's fiancé, Mike Schwartz.

"Sherlock," he replied. She grimaced. He knew she hated the nickname, and she suspected he continued to use it for that reason.

"Did you see what happened?" Riley looked over the interior of the car, taking in the long legs and short skirt of the very attractive young blonde woman in the passenger seat.

"No, there was some commotion and I saw the van go into the bridge barrier, flip, and then several cars rear-end one another. I was a ways back and stopped with plenty of room."

"Right. And you didn't see what caused the van to veer out of control?"

"No—"

"I didn't see anything either, except the stupid dog or whatever running over the road," the blonde added. Her voice was high-pitched and saccharine. Riley didn't know who she was, but she epitomized the sort of woman she found hard to respect, a woman who made herself small to be attractive to men.

"And what's your name, ma'am?"

"Cindy Cartwright," she said, then spelled both names so Riley could write them down.

"And you said there was a dog on the road?"

"Yes, I didn't see where it came from, but suddenly it was there in the middle of the road. I think the postal van tried to avoid it and then crashed."

"Can you describe the dog?"

"Not really, light brown maybe, very fast, jumping all over the place."

"Okay. And what is your relationship to Mister Schwartz?"

"He's my boyfriend," she said. Mike glared at her and started to talk over her.

"We work together, Sherlock, nothing exciting."

"Sorry, yes, Mike is my boss, Officer." Cindy blushed, her neck and cheeks turning a vivid shade of blotchy pink.

Riley couldn't help the eyebrow that arched up. "I see." She had always thought Mike was a conniving finance-bro who was hiding something, but had never had any evidence. Now she had him in a car with a woman who claimed he was her boyfriend.

"Petra doesn't need to know about this. Cindy's a colleague. We work together."

"And what is your purpose for being on the bridge at this time? In the middle of a workday."

"We had a client meeting on the mainland," Mike said. "We called to cancel when the van blocked the road."

"I hope you used the handsfree to make that call."

"No, I called," Cindy said, before Mike turned back to glare at her again.

He must behave differently with Petra. If he was like this around her, she would kick him to the curb in three seconds flat.

"Here's my business card." Riley handed one to both Mike and Cindy. "You may need to give a formal statement later, depending on how the investigation gets on. You can turn the car around and head back to the island. I expect the road will be blocked for some time until they can clear all this up."

"Thank you, Sergeant Holmes," Mike said. Riley waved him away.

You can use my name when you're sucking up then. Riley was incensed, not only that Mike had proven to be a lying piece of garbage—as much as she hadn't liked him, it was different now that her friend was being hurt—but also that he expected her not to tell Petra. On the other hand, Petra knew Riley didn't like Mike, and she worried that telling her about the interaction would make her seem petty.

Riley shook herself and brought her mind back to the job, canvassing the drivers before they all left the scene.

***

Petra arrived home to her cold and empty apartment. She lived alone. Mike would stay over a few nights a week, but they'd agreed not to move in together until after the wedding.

Not that he'll agree on a date. Petra sighed. A nice hot shower might help rejuvenate her. After spending time with Margaret to ease her passing, Petra felt drained and agitated.

Once showered, she flopped onto her bed, wearing only a purple towel, and stared at the ceiling. Her phone buzzed and she grabbed it.

I had a hectic day at work; just got off a twelve-hour shift. I'm making my

19

famous mac and cheese for dinner if you
want to join us.

It was from Riley, her best friend's sister, motorcycle
cop by day, and accomplished cook by night. It would be
nice to be around people she felt totally at ease with.

You're a lifesaver. That sounds
awesome. Just gotta change, be there in
fifteen minutes.

Petra's parents moved away from San Destino ten
years ago, when she was only seventeen. She'd lived on
her own ever since. Her parents had helped pay the rent
for a couple of years, maybe to relieve some of the guilt
of living off the island and refusing to visit her.

During those early years, Petra had spent most of her
time with Maddy, Riley's younger sister, and had become
a de facto part of their family. Riley was the eldest and
took care of everyone, especially after their mom's stroke
five years ago.

Petra's apartment was only a couple of blocks away
from the Holmes' and she usually walked there. Petra's
place wasn't in the best neighborhood, and she could
afford to look for somewhere a bit fancier now she had
started working in a couple of good jobs, but she still
preferred having her chosen family close in case of days
like today when their comfort would help restore her
energy.

She approached the Holmes' place—a two-story
Edwardian terrace house, with a protruding bay window

and a tiny porch with a swinging chair. It had definitely seen better days, the mauve paint peeling, the swing upholstery worn, but all three kids stayed there with their mom.

Riley moved back in after their dad died, then Maddy came back, while Jen had never left and played up being the baby of the family.

"Hey, you made it just in time," Riley said, her usually vibrant eyes shadowed by dark, purple-tinged rings, her posture more hunched.

"I would never pass up your cooking," Petra said, stepping forward to hug her. Riley gave some of the best hugs around, something about her strong arms, and gruff exterior made the tenderness of her hugs even better.

"Pets!" Maddy yelled, galumphing down the stairs in her gigantic shoes as always. There was very little subtlety to the middle Holmes girl. She wore very tight jeans, and all her shirts had tasteful holes cut in them. The style wasn't quite punk, but punk adjacent. Whereas Riley had a more refined style, preferring fitted trousers and button-down shirts, though today her shirt was wrinkled, perhaps a testament to her hectic shift.

Petra extricated herself from Maddy's hug. "Tell me about your day, Riley."

"Why? What happened today?" Maddy examined her nails.

"Let me get dinner out and I'll tell you both." Riley served out four portions. She would need to feed her mother, Georgina, later on, since she couldn't eat on her own.

Georgina had lost a lot of functions in recent years and needed help getting around. They'd moved her bed into the living room too, so she didn't have to do so many stairs. The stroke had taken most of her language and movement, but Georgina's mind was intact.

Petra would often sit with her, sometimes helping her eat, or just holding her hand and talking to her in her mind. She hadn't told any of the Holmes girls she had this talent. They'd probably tell her she was a weirdo, so it was just a secret between her and Georgina, her second mother.

"Smells amazing. Thanks for cooking, Riley," Petra said.

"Any time." Riley smiled and turned away. If Petra didn't know any better, she would have thought Riley was blushing.

Once the other plates were on the table, and everyone had sat down, Riley sighed.

"What happened at work?" Petra asked.

"Did you hear about the accident on the bridge?"

"There was an accident?" Maddy said.

"Yeah, the postal van overturned. Full blockage of four lanes right in the middle of peak hour. I was the first on scene. There weren't too many injuries, but it was a real shit show—debris, letters, and flowers. A florist's van got busted up too, stuff all over the place. I had to hang around for ages while they cleaned it up to manage traffic."

"I thought you were home late today," Maddy said.

"Yeah, it's good overtime though." Riley smiled, but it didn't lift the fatigue on her face.

"Did something else happen?" The feeling of quiet despair coming off Riley didn't seem to match the description she'd just given.

Riley's fork paused half-way to her mouth. "Mike was on the bridge."

"Oh my god, is he okay? Was he injured?"

"No, he's fine, didn't even ding the Porsche." Again, that joyless smile.

"But?" Maddy prompted.

"I shouldn't say anything," Riley replied.

"About what? You can't stop there," Maddy said.

Riley put her fork down and scrubbed her hands over her face, then through her hair. "He was in the car with Cindy, from his office."

"I know Cindy," Petra said, a cold ball of fear forming in her belly. "She seems nice." *For a vacuous secretarial type.*

"Isn't she the blonde you said you got weird vibes off?" Maddy asked.

"Yeah. When I dropped something to Mike at the office a couple of months ago. She was nice enough, but it felt like she pitied me, said that she would put in a good word for me if I wanted a real job, as if I'd want to work in an office all day."

"What does she do there?" Riley asked.

I don't know where this is going, and I don't like it. "She's a clerk of some sort, or maybe admin. Is that important?"

"I don't know. They said they were going to see a client on the mainland."

"That's probably true. I don't know what he does most of the time. He's told me what his job involves, but it sounds very dull."

"You don't think it was a client meeting, do you?" Maddy said, her eyebrows raised in question.

"I…" Riley trailed off.

"What aren't you saying?" Petra stared hard at Riley.

"When I asked how Cindy knew Mike, she said he was her boyfriend."

"You're making that up."

"Why would she be making that up? When has Riley ever lied to you?" Maddy's voice rose with anger.

"I knew you were jealous of my engagement, Ri, but this is low. I thought you were better than this." Petra dropped her fork, which clattered against the plate. She stood, grabbed her bag, and stormed out of the house without another word.

She marched all the way back to her apartment building, but was still so angry that she kept walking, not paying attention to where she was going. It was dark, but the weather was mild. The stars looked down on her emotional turmoil indifferent.

If Riley was right, and Cindy and Mike were—she couldn't bear to even think it—more than friends, her life was built on a lie. She'd been with him since they met in college. He'd pursued her, he'd been the one making big decisions, and she'd gone with the flow.

When he asked her to marry him on their fourth anniversary, she said yes. Not because she had always dreamed of being a wife, she didn't care about a piece of paper or a big ceremony, but because she knew it meant something to him. He needed the piece of paper, he wanted the big wedding, and she wanted him to be happy.

But what if he was cheating with some young blonde from his office? He did spend a lot of time there, and he never liked sleeping over, but that was because he had restless leg syndrome. It was the most cliched thing he could have done, and he hadn't even turned thirty yet. It couldn't be true. It couldn't be.

She reached the houseboats around Kismet Bay, a mile or so from her building. Petra's skin prickled as the wind off the water caught her.

What if Riley was the one lying? She'd known her since they were kids. The Holmes were more like her family than her own parents.

Yes, Riley had been a bit weird a few times. Petra had started to think maybe her best friend's sister had feelings for her, but she must know Petra didn't think of her like that.

Why would she lie? Being the bearer of such devastating news, especially if it wasn't true, would ruin their friendship, and push Petra away perhaps forever. She wouldn't risk that. No way. So maybe Riley was mistaken.

Yes, that must be it. She'd misunderstood what was happening, and trying to be a good friend, had told Petra. She would have a chat with Mike about it, clear the air, and explain it all to Riley.

Petra looked at her watch—already after nine o'clock and she was still sitting by the water, getting cold. After a long day, a patient death, and an interrupted dinner, Petra wanted nothing more than to climb into bed and sleep for at least two days. Too bad she had to work again tomorrow.

Better get home. She turned and started back up the hill, her aching feet protesting.

Chapter 2

Riley watched Petra walk out and felt as though her heart was breaking. The front door slammed behind Petra's flash of retreating flame-red hair, and she jumped.

"Why did you say that?" Maddy asked, her tone hard and accusatory.

"You think I should have kept the info to myself?"

"Yes! Why would she want to know her fiancé is cheating with his secretary?"

"I know this is hard for you to understand, but you can't be in a relationship with a liar. No matter what else is going on, truth, loyalty, those are the things that can't be compromised."

"This is why you're single. All men cheat, it's just the way of the world. Petra would have been happier not knowing, and now you've ruined her relationship over nothing. And possibly your friendship too."

"What are you talking about?" Riley frowned. "Dad never cheated."

Maddy raised an eyebrow and said nothing.

"What does that mean?"

"Why? So you can know the truth and be miserable like Petra?"

"Does Mom know?" Riley dropped her voice, hoping that her mother couldn't hear their conversation from the other room.

"Everyone except you knows, Riley. It's the worst kept secret in the family. You only think he's a good guy because you were too busy mooning over Petra to see what was going on under your nose."

"I was not." Riley stood ramrod straight. Her little sister had never spoken to her like this before. Where had all this anger come from? Maddy was shaking with rage.

"Mom knew the score. Dad would stay at work late a couple of nights a month. A woman called here for him one time, said she was his secretary, but when I called him to the phone he was so mad—not at me, at her, for calling the house. He did that angry whisper down the line as though I couldn't hear everything he said. Jen even caught him hugging some young thing outside his office once when she went to surprise him for lunch on summer break."

Riley was stunned. Her mouth hung open as though searching for the words to respond.

"Men have needs. They want to spread their seed around, but they want their secure home too. Petra is wife material; someone you can rely on to keep things running at home, but most dudes need excitement, the thrill of the chase, as well as security."

"Who are you? When did you become so fucking cynical?"

Maddy picked up her fork and went back to her meal. "Dean and I have an unspoken arrangement. He does what he needs to do, I don't ask him any questions. One day, if there's a hot dude in my office, I might dabble, but we know it doesn't mean anything. I'm his rock, the one he'll always come back to."

"You knew about Mike?"

"Of course, I knew. Cindy isn't the first, and won't be the last, I'm sure." Maddy chewed the mac and cheese with such a smug look on her face, Riley couldn't stand to stay in the room any longer.

"I don't know what happened, but I feel sorry for you if that's what you think love is." Riley turned away and ran upstairs to her bedroom, her refuge in the attic.

They had renovated when she moved back in. She wanted to cry, for Maddy, for Petra, for her mom, but the tears wouldn't come. She was filled with white hot rage at all the men who treated women like property, the lying, cheating, scumbags. *Thank God I'm not attracted to men.*

***

The next morning when Riley woke up it took several minutes to remember the terrible fight she'd had with a woman she'd loved for years. She wasn't in love with Petra, that would be inappropriate, she loved her more like an extra sister.

Riley didn't have to go on shift until two that afternoon, and she dreaded going downstairs in case she ran into Jen or Maddy. She couldn't handle any more revelations about her world right now.

In the end, hunger won out, Riley's belly rumbled and the only solution was to go down to the kitchen. With all the drama last night, she had barely eaten.

I wonder if anyone put the mac and cheese in the fridge, or if it sat out getting spoiled.

She walked down the stairs, the first floor empty, both her sisters likely at work. As Riley stepped off the staircase on the ground floor, her was mother bent over awkwardly in her chair.

"Shit, Mom, have you been here all night?" Riley rushed to her mother's chair and helped her to sit up straight again. Her mother's eyes shone, as though she wanted to cry, but she hadn't been able to speak much for a long time.

"I'm so sorry I didn't check on you before I went to sleep. Jen and Maddy were both home. Did they look in before they went to bed? Or before they went to work?"

Georgina's eyes closed slowly, and there was a sadness in her face, despite the paralysis.

"I'll fucking kill them." Riley clenched her teeth. "Sorry, language, I know." She tried to smile, but it felt forced. They had hired a nurse to come every day and shower Georgina—she had her own keys, and let herself in if all the daughters were out.

Riley could smell the need for her mother's continence underwear to be changed. Usually, one of them would do it last thing at night and first thing in the morning at least.

"Why does it have to be me that keeps this family together?" Riley said. "Okay, Mom, we need to get you into some clean things, and then I'll bring you some breakfast."

The mac and cheese still sat on the dining table, just where it had been left last night. Maddy's plate lay bare—clearly she hadn't been too upset to eat—and she'd left it there for Riley to deal with.

"You'd say I shouldn't be too hard on Maddy, she's had a tough time, but I've had it just as tough. I don't go around making excuses for creeps." Riley sighed. "Did Dad really do all that stuff she said?"

Georgina didn't weigh much these days, but Riley still used the ergonomic lift aid the nursing agency had brought whenever she transferred her mother from the chair to the bed and back.

"I'm so sorry. I didn't know. You never said anything. I thought you two were happy. I guess maybe you were, in a manner of speaking. But you can't believe you deserved that, do you Mom?" Riley had moved her mother onto the bed and began the process of cleaning her up and changing her clothes and continence aid. She was as tender as she could be, her mother's skin red and angry from sitting in urine all night.

"You're all raw, I'm sorry. I'll put some ointment on, it might sting." Riley talked her mother through what she was doing as she went. Her mom's mind was still in there, as far as the doctors could figure out. It was just her body that didn't respond the way it used to.

"Do you want something to eat? Or no?" Riley asked.

Georgina mumbled something that sounded like *no*.

"I'll leave you to get some rest, I'll check on you in a bit."

Once Georgina was comfortable on the bed and could maybe get some proper sleep, Riley went into the dining room and cleared all the dishes from the night before. She clenched her teeth, muttering under her breath about her lazy, thoughtless little sisters.

Riley often had eggs for breakfast, but she didn't have the energy for cooking, and found some cereal in the cupboard, chocolate something or other that Jen would have bought. She was never very good at eating well, that one.

She sat at the now clean dining table, and Riley heard her mother's soft breathing in the other room, hoping she rested well.

Her thoughts went back to Petra. She'd walked out of the house, life as she knew it possibly in tatters, and Riley hadn't checked on her.

I might not even be welcome if I dropped around. Riley stared glumly at the brown tinted milk in the bottom of her bowl. But if she didn't try, she'd be angrier at herself than she was already.

She looked in on her mother, her eyes were open. "I'm gonna shower, Mom. You okay?"

Georgina gave a semblance of a nod, and Riley went back upstairs to get ready to go out. She was on shift later, so would need to have her kit and uniform with her. After a brief, but thorough shower, she combed her short dark hair, parting it just so on the left side.

"How do I look?" Riley said, reentering the lounge-cum-bedroom on the ground floor. One side of her mother's mouth tugged up in a smile, and she moaned in a positive tone.

"Good, you reckon?" Riley turned around to show her mom the back. "I'm going to see if Petra will talk to me."

Georgina grumbled.

"I know, I messed up. She wasn't ready to hear what I had to say about Mike. But Maddy didn't help either. Not everyone cheats. I can't bear to think of Petra being legally bound to a man who thinks he can bang whoever he pleases. She deserves better."

Georgina's eyes twitched.

"Don't you start. We're just friends. I know she's not into women, and she's like my sister." *Keep telling yourself that.* "Will you be all right until Emma gets here later?"

Her mom nodded, or at least what they had come to understand was a nod with her impaired movement.

"Do you need help back into the chair?"

Georgina shook her head.

"I love you, Mom. I'm gonna have words with those other two for leaving you like that last night. They know better."

If Riley hadn't known better, she would have sworn she heard her mother say *thank you.*

***

Riley took her own motorcycle, a bulky, noisy, black hog, to Petra's apartment building a few blocks away, her work kit in a duffle bag strapped over her shoulder.

She parked on the pavement in front and buzzed Petra's apartment. The small block was a little worse for wear but structurally sound. At least it had a security entrance—Bloomington was a bit sketchy in some areas.

She should be home, I don't think she's working today. Riley waited for Petra's usually sparkling, sweet voice to come over the tinny speaker.

"What do you want?" The security camera meant Petra could see who had buzzed. She didn't seem happy.

"I want to apologize. Can I come up?"

A sigh sounded through the speaker, followed by a crackly buzz as Petra let her in.

Riley's heart pounded in her chest. *She let me in. That's a good start.*

Petra's small, organized apartment was decorated in muted neutral tones with splashes of terra cotta, sage, and forest green. Riley had always found the décor soothing, but today even that couldn't calm the butterflies in her stomach.

"Alright, you're here." Petra's eyes were puffy, and she looked even paler than usual, her arms wrapped around herself, leaning on her dining table. Her unruly flame-red hair was sticking out of a big messy bun.

We're not getting comfortable, better get straight to it. "I'm sorry."

"Really? What for?"

"I'm sorry I told you about Mike and Cindy. I'm sorry Maddy behaved like a spoiled child. I should have told you in private. I could have presented what I saw differently."

Petra held her mouth in a small, tight line but stayed silent.

"I didn't mean to hurt you," Riley continued. "I thought you deserved to know. I didn't think about how it would potentially mess everything up."

"I was so mad last night."

"I know. I'm so sorry."

Petra put her hand up, and Riley shut her mouth, giving Petra space to say what she needed to.

"I left your place, and I walked down to Kismet Cove. I wanted to get away from you, but maybe also to get away from myself. It didn't work."

Riley thought she saw a hint of a smile through the sorrow on Petra's face.

"I got back here and barely slept. I woke up at six and texted Mike to ask him to call me as soon as he woke up." She sighed and rubbed her hand over her eyes. Riley wanted more than anything to comfort her, hug her and tell her it would be okay, but it wasn't the time.

"He called at eight thirty, driving to work, didn't think it was urgent enough to interrupt his morning routine." Petra scoffed. "I asked him who Cindy was. He said they worked together. I asked if they were sleeping together. He said *no*. But—"

Riley thought Petra might cry, but instead she took a trembling breath and continued.

"But it was the way he said *no*. I can tell when he's lying. Sure, I didn't know he wasn't being faithful, but I never had cause to ask him outright. Half-truths, and lying by omission sometimes slip past me if I'm not concentrating, but when someone lies to my face, so to speak, I know. Although maybe it's not so reliable with people I'm close to."

Riley had always known Petra knew things she shouldn't. Her work with the dying always seemed sort of sacred, mystical.

"I know you weren't lying last night, as much as that would have been easier. It's part of why I was so upset. You could have been mistaken. If people think they're telling the truth I don't see a lie, but you weren't lying."

"I'm so sorry," Riley said after a lengthy pause.

"I can't stay with him now. It's all come crashing down. The life I thought I'd have. I guess in hindsight not moving in together makes more sense…" She dropped her arms and crumpled on herself. All the strength she'd used to hold herself up against the weight of Mike's betrayal had dissipated.

"Let's sit down," Riley said, holding her arms out as though to shepherd her to the couch. Petra allowed herself to be guided. Riley had never seen her so deflated. "I don't know if you want to hear this, but he doesn't deserve your loyalty."

Petra lifted her red-rimmed eyes. Her lower lip began to tremble. "I know." She sobbed once, and the tears she'd been holding back flowed over her cheeks.

She looked so small and fragile. So lost. Riley, on the other end of the couch, put one hand on Petra's knee, and she curled into a ball, laying her head on Riley's leg.

Riley stroked her hair in silence until she had stopped crying, all the while trying to tamp down the urge to wrap her in her arms and kiss away the tears. *It isn't the time. Petra doesn't feel the same.*

"Do you have to go on shift soon?" Petra asked.

"Yeah, I brought my uniform with me." Riley inclined her head to the bag she'd left on the floor near the front door. "I need to go in about half an hour, but I can stay here till then if you want me to."

"I'd like that." Petra pushed herself into a seated position and shuffled back over to her side of the couch. "I'm gonna go tidy myself up a bit."

Riley nodded, and watched her walk away, still sad, but now moving with purpose. A few minutes passed, she heard water running, and closet doors opening.

Eventually Petra returned. She had put some make-up on, her eyes looked less like she'd been crying, and she'd changed her outfit into a smart, tailored linen suit that made her look powerful, purposeful.

"Can you do me a favor?"

"Anything," Riley replied, in awe of the strength she must have to get herself together so quickly.

"Can you take me to Mike's building on your way to the station? I'm giving the ring back."

Riley's mouth tugged up in a half smile. "Sure. You look like a million bucks. He'll be sorry he let you go."

"He better be." Petra picked up her handbag and strode to the door.

Chapter 3

Petra looked at the enormous sapphire, surrounded by small diamonds in a white gold setting that Mike had given her when they got engaged, as she and Riley walked out of the building.

Petra had so many emotions swirling around inside her, most of them anger and sadness about Mike, but there was a sense of relief too. As though somewhere inside, way down where she didn't look, where she kept her feelings about her parents, she had known Mike wasn't meant to be her soul mate. Sure, he was hot, and rich, but he was smug, elitist, and rude to wait staff. That sort of thing never boded well.

He'd been so kind at the start. With her parents being out of the picture and feeling lost, she had basked in the attention of an attractive, attentive man. Slowly he'd revealed himself to be shallow, manipulative, and dismissive of her needs, but he always had an excuse— work was stressful, he hadn't meant it, or he would promise to be better next time. Maddy said she was loyal to a fault. Maybe this is what she meant.

"I don't have a spare helmet," Riley said as they stopped by her motorbike on the pavement. "You'll have to wear mine."

"No, that's okay. I don't want to put you out. I asked for the lift."

"I insist. My bike, my rules." Riley's face set in her not-in-the-mood-for–arguing expression.

"Okay." Petra pulled the long, acrylic hairpin out of her bun so the helmet would sit properly. She shook out her hair and tucked it into the collar of her blazer so it wouldn't whip around and blind her or Riley.

Riley straddled the bike. Her well-muscled thighs looked so powerful as she held it steady so Petra could climb on behind. She had ridden like this a few times before, though usually when they traveled anywhere together Maddy and Jen would be there and take a car.

Riley started the engine and the bike vibrated.

She tried to maintain a respectful gap between her groin and Riley's behind, but as soon as they rolled over the curb onto the road, she slipped forward and found herself pressed against Riley. Something about the warm, powerful curves stirred a feeling in Petra's groin she hadn't experienced for a while.

Stop it, she's like your sister. She tried to shift back up the bike's seat.

"Keep still," Riley said, turning her head a little so she could keep her eyes on the road while talking to her.

"Sorry." Petra stopped fidgeting and tried not to think about what, or who, was between her legs. Best not to distract the driver when she was wearing Riley's only helmet.

Mike's office building was on the edge of Pinnacle Plaza, near the business district—a tall glass office building, one of the newest in San Destino, he had told her with pride.

Riley pulled the bike up onto the pavement, and turned off the motor before they both dismounted.

"Do I have helmet hair?" Petra pulled her head free and handed the helmet back to Riley.

"You look fantastic, as you always do." Riley put the helmet on the bike's seat, and when she turned back, her face was serious again. "You don't have to do anything rash. I know you're upset, but you can take a day or two to consider things."

Petra looked down at the ring again and pulled it off her finger. "I don't need to think about it. I'm not sad to end things, I'm upset because I was so blind. So caught up in the fiction of our happily ever after that I brushed everything wrong with Mike away. He's a dick, he's always been that way, and I'd rather be single than stuck with him till death do us part."

Riley smiled. "You've always been strong. I admire that about you. I know you're hurting now, but I think it's the right decision. Not that my opinion matters, I'm just—"

"You're a good friend. Thank you for the ride. I know it was out of your way." Petra hugged Riley, pulling her close and feeling the firmness of her body against her own. She lingered for a little too long and had to force herself to let go. "You have to get to work."

"Yes. Text me how it went. So I know not to worry."

"You don't have to be my mom too. You have enough to take care of with your own family as it is."

"Can't help it." Riley's cheeks reddened and she looked away.

"Ride safe," Petra said, as Riley mounted the bike and started it up.

Riley pushed the helmet on, nodded, and took off down the street toward Stonehaven and the police station.

Now she was alone, Petra worried she'd chicken out of what she'd come to do…until she looked up and saw Cindy walking toward her carrying several of those enormous, expensive coffees Mike and his finance buddies loved.

"Hey Cindy," she said, walking toward the slim blonde woman.

"Oh… hey." Cindy frowned.

"It's Petra, you know, Mike's fiancée."

"Of course, sorry. Your face was familiar, but I couldn't place you."

"All good."

"Are you coming up? The guys are in meetings all day. That's why I got sent out for these." She waved the coffees in Petra's direction.

"Yeah, I need to have a word with Mike. As soon as possible."

Cindy's walk faltered for a moment. "Follow me, but I don't think I'll be able to convince him to come out."

"Let's see if I can persuade him." *That slimeball better speak to me after that obvious lie this morning. He should be groveling.*

The two women rode the elevator in silence to the tenth floor. They were the largest hedge fund in San Destino, possibly one of the biggest in California, if Mike was to be believed. The doors opened onto the flashy chrome and frosted glass reception area, where Cindy usually worked, however, it had been left unattended while she went out for their beverages.

"Just wait here, please. I'll see if Mike can see you."

"Thanks." Petra sat on an architecturally interesting black and chrome chair that wasn't comfortable in the slightest.

Mike's office had always given her the creeps, to the point where she couldn't wait to leave. This time she would be leaving permanently, without the enormous engagement ring.

Several minutes later, Cindy came back out, her brow furrowed and her eyes tense. "Mike said he can't see you today."

Petra stood, taking time to make herself appear as calm yet furious as she could. "I know about you two. He probably didn't mention that—"

Cindy opened her mouth, but Petra put her hand up to interrupt.

"My friend Riley, the police sergeant you encountered yesterday on the bridge, told me what she saw, and Mike was fool enough this morning to confirm it. Tell him he needs to see me right now, or I'll have to give the message to you. Can you do that please?" Petra kept her voice low, quiet, and, she hoped, terrifying. Cindy deserved it, having known Mike was in a relationship.

"Um. Okay." Cindy scurried back through the doors into the secret inner sanctum of the finance office.

Petra had never been beyond the reception area. She had avoided visiting Mike at work, and when she had, was never invited past the waiting area.

When Cindy returned, after a few minutes, she looked even paler than before. Her hands, with their absurdly long acrylic nails, were clasped in front of her so tightly her fingers had turned blue-white.

"He said he can't come out."

"I see." Petra sighed, opened her hand, and held out the engagement ring. "Will you take this to him, please?"

Cindy nodded and took the ring, her mouth curled down in distaste.

"Tell him we're done. I want nothing more to do with him. If he has any property of mine at his place, he can mail it to me. If I find anything of his, I'll do the same. You can also tell him I think he's a spineless, selfish, piece of shit and I hope he's miserable."

"I'm so sorry. I didn't know he was engaged when it started, and then after I found out, he assured me you two were in the process of breaking up."

"I really don't care. Sleeping with your boss is a bad move no matter the situation."

Petra turned to leave but thought better of it.

"You're the sort of person he preys on. He's got a lot of money, a flashy car, and nice clothes, but all of that is window dressing to cover the fact he's a terrible person. He won't be faithful to you either; a cheater is a cheater. If he promised you promotions or a career, he won't follow through. He's using you for sex. He doesn't respect you."

Cindy's mouth worked up and down as she fumbled to formulate a response.

Petra turned back to the elevator and was annoyed to have to wait for it, while Cindy stood silently watching her.

Some dramatic exit this was.

Back on the pavement outside the shiny, glass office building, Petra suddenly felt very alone. She hadn't been single for a long time. She'd started dating Mike five years ago. He proposed on their fourth anniversary as though it was just something they should do. She said yes because she couldn't see any reason not to.

Since her parents moved away from San Destino, she had craved stability. Petra dated her high school sweetheart, Jared, from sophomore year until he graduated college and moved to Seattle for work.

She'd had a couple of dalliances between Jared and Mike, and Maddy once accused her of serial monogamy and when she met Mike, jumped into the relationship with him.

The things she'd found charming at first, his need for status, the desire to climb the corporate ladder, and his pathological need to impress his parents became more and more burdensome.

Her job wasn't good enough for him—she was a freelance yoga teacher, which had no clear career progression, or the possibility of making huge piles of cash. Unambitious is what he'd said, but Petra knew he meant lazy.

Petra had lived with her frail grandmother after her parents left. The Holmes family stepped in to help, right when her nanna was coming to the end of her life. It all happened just before finals in junior year, that Petra discovered her other abilities.

Her grandmother couldn't really talk, and when she did, it didn't always make sense, but if Petra held her hand and concentrated, she could understand what Nanna said without hearing her speak the words.

Sometimes it came to her in images. For a while it was all jumbled, but Petra got better at it, maybe Nanna did too, and they found a way to have whole conversations without speaking.

Nanna died while Petra held her hand. They both knew it was time, and Petra concentrated hard on making her grandmother comfortable, speeding her to the other side, wherever that was. It didn't seem like much, but she hoped it helped.

After that, the home asked her if she would help with the other patients who were confused, or found it hard to communicate. Petra would sit with them, hold their hand, and they would muddle their way through together until they figured out how to talk to one another. Each person was different, but in some ways, it was the same. Petra never explained it to anyone, and no one ever asked.

When Georgina Holmes had had her last stroke, a big one this time, Petra had to work especially hard to find the connection. It was like trying to untangle a mass of wires, the usual routes she took blocked off. It took a few weeks, but they got there in the end. By that time, Georgina was almost crying with frustration, her mouth refusing to form words, and if she did, they sounded meaningless.

Why was Petra thinking about Nanna, and Jared, and Georgina right now? Perhaps she was clinging to anything that might reassure her she wasn't alone, that she was loved. But it didn't help.

I'll go and have a chat with a couple of the residents. It might be tiring, but at least it feels like I'm doing something important, instead of standing here, watching the world go past. It's not like Mike will come out after me.

The thought Mike didn't even care enough to chase her was equal parts humiliating and liberating. She'd made the right decision, even if it felt awful right now.

***

Riley arrived at the station feeling a little better, but still pretty crappy. Petra had forgiven her, but the fact remained she had caused her to break off her engagement.

No, Mike did that. Though, knowing it was true didn't make her feel any better.

"Sherlock," Watch Commander Ward said as she came out for roll call. A short, burly, ginger-haired man in his late forties, his pale skin had permanently reddened from being in the sun.

"Sir," she said, nodding her head. She wished they had never come up with that nickname.

"You'll be with a rookie today. We don't have any training officers available."

"I'm not a TO. You can't put me with a rookie." To her own ears she sounded whiny. It wasn't her intention, but the fact remained she had never qualified as a TO, and it wasn't fair, or safe, to put a rookie with her.

"That's true, but you've sat the exam, and you got damn close. You have the knowledge, and I don't have anyone else to keep an eye on this one." Ward inclined his head to a short, petite man who didn't look old enough to have completed basic training.

"And," Ward said before Riley could make any further protests, "he's had three weeks already with Simmons. He's not as useless as he looks, are you, rookie?"

The rookie's face reddened. At least Riley's annoying nickname wasn't based on her physical appearance, or her gender, which was a blessing.

"Yes, sir."

"This is Officer Jason Bell. He'll be assigned to a car with you today."

Of course, rookies aren't allowed on bikes. "Yes, sir," she replied.

"Rookie, this is your TO, Sergeant Riley Holmes. Everyone calls her Sherlock."

Riley tried not to grimace.

"Sergeant Holmes, it's a pleasure to meet you." Bell held out his hand to shake hers. He was awkwardly formal, perhaps trying to make a good impression, despite his clear anxiety—hunched shoulders, arms folded around his torso as though for comfort, and barely taking his eyes off the floor.

"Alright, let's get this show on the road." Riley turned and walked toward the equipment bay to collect their weapons and other materials to stock the vehicle. It had been at least six months since she'd been in a car, and she'd never trained a rookie. She hoped this guy was sensible and wouldn't put himself in harm's way.

"And call me Holmes, or Riley, when we're out today."

"Yes, ma'am."

"And no ma'am okay?"

"Uuh, okay."

They did their start-of-shift checks, then Riley slid in behind the wheel of the police vehicle. She pulled into traffic and headed out to patrol. She was a beat cop and had been for years. For a while, she'd wanted to be a detective, but when her dad died, and then her mom got sick, it wasn't worth the disruption to her hours to go for the promotion.

Detectives had crazy hours. At least on patrol, even with night shifts, she would have days at a time scheduled off and she would be able to care for her mom.

"Do you have a nickname yet?" Riley glanced briefly at her companion.

"I do, and I don't like it any better than you like Sherlock."

"I see." Riley said nothing more and the pause stretched out. She knew how to use silence to create intimacy, or in this case, discomfort.

"It's Tinkerbell."

"Ah." *A play on both his name and his stature. That would definitely stick. Poor guy.* "Damn. Mine is just the prototype for a great detective, so y'know, no pressure." From the corner of her eye, Riley thought she saw Bell's mouth twitch in a smile. The silence after that merged into something more comfortable.

Occasionally the radio burbled with calls, but none were for them, or in their area, so she just drove down to the waterfront and parked the car with a good view of the boutiques along the shopping strip at the end of Providence Pier.

When she'd driven past Destiny Bridge on the way in, Riley had been glad to see traffic flowing. The accident from the day before had all been cleared up.

The shift started at two that afternoon and ended at midnight. Their station ran three ten-hour shifts to cover morning, afternoon and night shift.

Riley liked it better than the twelve-hour shifts she'd had to do when she covered a few weeks in Los Angeles during the Superbowl. Working in LA had been intense. So many people, so many different areas, and even with a local partner, she'd felt useless and hokey.

Outside of San Destino there was a kind of dullness to the sound, as though she could never hear as clearly as she did at home. Riley didn't believe the stories about psychic powers, or paranormal stuff happening in her home town, though most people did. She had chalked it up to local knowledge making her brain work more effectively, but it wasn't a satisfactory answer.

"Have you ever had something weird happen on a shift?" Bell said, as though he'd been reading her mind. Or possibly she'd been reading his while he formulated the question.

"What sort of weird?"

"I've lived in San Destino my whole life and there have always been things that were hard to explain…"

"Yeah. I've had a few strange shifts. Nothing that crossed the realm of scientific possibility, but the sort of thing you would expect to happen once in a million, and then you see it like, three weeks in a row, y'know?"

"Oh, I meant like, objects moving when they shouldn't or seeing a ghost."

Riley laughed. "I've never had that happen." She thought for a moment. "One time, when I was out on the bike, on my own, I was called to a vehicle collision. I was first on scene, a car t-boned by a pickup truck.

"The pickup driver and his passenger were a bit banged up, but generally okay. I told them to stay in the vehicle until the paramedics arrived, but the woman driving the car was in bad shape." The scene had been hard to look at when she arrived.

"I was sure she was dead. No one could survive that, but I had to check. I reached in through the broken driver's side window, felt for a pulse on the wrist— nothing, neck—nothing. I couldn't do CPR, she was pretty…mangled. I just stood there till the paramedics arrived."

"That sounds awful, but pretty standard so far."

"I'm getting to it. The medics arrived, and we all went straight to the woman in the car. I told them I couldn't find a pulse, and one of the paramedics said he'd check her again just in case.

"He pulled off his glove and laid his bare hand on her forehead for a full ten seconds, eyes closed. His mouth moved a little, but he didn't say anything, I figured he'd said a prayer or something, you know, to send her off to wherever we go after we die—"

"And then what?" Bell interrupted.

Riley turned to look at her rookie and he sat forward in the passenger seat, eyes wide and eager. "He put the glove back on, and checked her neck again, and I swear to god this woman who was dead for a good five minutes came back to life."

"No way!"

"I'm serious. She had no pulse and wasn't breathing as far as I could tell, until this guy said a prayer over her, or whatever he did."

"Did she make it?"

"They rushed her to hospital and she had a crushed leg, broken ribs, head trauma, the works. I didn't expect she'd pull through, but then a few years later, I pulled over a decrepit looking blue sedan with only one taillight, and it was her."

"No."

"Yes. And she had recovered pretty well. Had some gnarly scars on her face, and she limped a little when I asked her out of the vehicle to do a field sobriety test."

"A paramedic who brings people back from the dead. I would not have expected that." Bell stared over the water, and Riley turned her attention back to watching the foot traffic and the shops.

"Most likely she wasn't dead, just had a very weak pulse and shallow breathing. The paramedic's touch probably did nothing, but that's the weirdest thing I've seen on the job."

"Right."

Dispatch came over the radio a few times, but nothing for them to action. The boutique area late on a Friday afternoon was pretty slow, usually. Sometimes in the evening it livened up, some of the trendy bars were hot spots for underage drinking, and occasionally they needed help with security issues.

For a while, a purse snatcher had worked the bars, but in recent times it had stopped.

"Four-Adam-ten, come in." A staticky female voice came over the radio.

"Four-Adam-ten, go ahead," Riley responded into the radio.

"We've got a four-one-five in progress outside *Bebidas*. Can you attend?"

"Ten-four, show us responding." Riley put the radio mic back onto its cradle and started up the car. Four-one-five was a disturbance, probably a drunk refusing to leave the area.

"It's early for a drunk call," Bell said.

"It might be something else."

"It's never anything else." Bell's voice was flat, and Riley glanced over.

"How can you be so young and yet so cynical?" She chuckled to herself. He would learn as he went through his training that the monotony of the job is what you looked forward to. The exciting stuff, that was dangerous.

A drunk who didn't like the fact the bar had cut them off was a specific type of problem that she was equipped to handle, but when they had to respond to someone who was out of their mind of bath salts, or an altercation with a partner, or both, that stuff escalated very quickly.

Riley steered the police cruiser to the end of the pier and parked. As she and Bell exited the car, a shrill scream pierced the air. Incoherent, high-pitched, probably female.

The pier wasn't too busy at this time of day, a few tourist-types perusing the market stalls, though they would be crawling later that night and on the weekend. A couple of old fellas fishing over one side, though their attention focused on the screaming match rather than their rods.

One stall holder smiled and nodded as they passed, as though to say he was glad someone with authority had arrived.

Outside the bar, which wouldn't open until later that day, a tall, slim dark-haired woman engaged in a loud disagreement with a muscular, shirtless blond man.

"What are you trying to pull here?" the man yelled at the woman, whose back was to Riley and Bell.

"That money's mine. I earned it," the woman screamed back. Something in her voice sounded familiar to Riley.

"Great, now the pigs are involved," the man said, as he spotted the two of them approaching.

"Is there a problem here?" Riley said. She and Bell stood on either side of the two having the fight, careful to stay out of grabbing or striking range, for the time being.

"What're you doing here?" the woman said, turning to Riley. Her ex-girlfriend, Janice. *Shit*.

"No one wants you here Ri. Just fuck off home, okay?"

"I can't do that." Riley took half a step forward. "People are concerned about your safety, so we need to lower our voices and see if we can't work things out."

"You know her?" Bell asked.

"Long story."

"Not really," Janice said, her mouth contorted in an intoxicated sneer. "You're a dud lay, and I dumped your ass."

"You're gay now, are you?" the man said.

"That's not our concern right now." Riley could feel this unraveling already. Janice had a history of drug and alcohol abuse, as well as a couple of arrests for prostitution. "The lady says you owe her money. Is that true?"

"No way. I never agreed to that."

"And you, Janice, what's your point of view?" Riley asked.

"It was a misunderstanding."

"I see. Officer Bell, what's your assessment of the situation?" Riley was curious to see whether Bell had come to the same conclusion she had, that this man was trying to get out of paying Janice for something, most likely drugs or sex.

"If you ask me, these two are very keen for us to be elsewhere, so whatever the money relates to, I suspect it's not what they would want police to know about. My guess is that a sex act took place and the gentlemen is reneging on his end of the agreement." Bell turned to Riley. "Do we have cause to search them?"

"Since they're both saying there's no problem, no. Take down this guy's details, in case we need them later, I'll have a word with Janice."

Janice scrunched up her nose and stepped back. Riley put a hand on her shoulder and walked her along the pier, out of earshot of Bell. "Did he try to skip out on paying for your time?"

"It's not like that," Janice said, lighting a cigarette, her shoulders hunched. "He's my boyfriend's brother. I did a favor for him, delivered some items. One of the items is defective, according to the buyer, and he refused to pay for it, so now Dylan won't pay for the delivery."

"I see," Riley said. It could be drugs, but it could be hot phones or anything, really. "How much does he owe you?"

"Seven hundred."

"For one job? Jeez, you're doing well." The likelihood the deal was illegal increased given how much she was getting paid to be the courier. "Have you got the defective item?"

Janice looked at Riley, her eyes widening.

"I'll take that as a yes. If we leave, will you be safe? Is Dylan going to hurt you if you give him the item back and forget about the money?"

"I'll never work for him again, but he won't beat me. You can go."

"I'm taking your word for this, because I know you, Janice, and I don't trust that guy at all. Maybe it's better if you don't work for him anymore."

"I can take care of myself, thanks." Janice folded her arms across her chest and pouted, anger simmering.

"I know you can. It was just a suggestion." Riley glanced at Bell who made his way toward them, while the man headed back to the shore. "Do you still have my number?"

"Yeah, probably. Why?"

"If you ever want me to come and help you out if stuff gets… intense or whatever, call me, okay?"

"Sure, but now you're a cop. Why would I trust you?"

Riley sighed. There were a lot of people who abused their power within law enforcement, and then there was all the systemic stuff on top of that making it hard for a lot of people to trust or feel safe around police. "I'm a human being first, police second. If you call me as a friend, I'll come."

Janice frowned, not convinced. "If I get in a jam, I'll call."

"Good."

"He seems…pleasant," Bell said.

"Did you get his details?" Riley asked.

"Yep. All here." Bell tapped his small black notepad.

"Looks like everything is sorted for the moment. Want us to drop you off somewhere?" Riley turned to Janice.

"I need a ride in a cop car like I need a hole in the head. Thanks all the same." At least Janice smiled as she said it, her posture straightening, and she seemed less jumpy now Dylan had left the vicinity.

Riley and Bell hung back on the boardwalk for a while, watching her walk away. Riley called in to dispatch to update them that the disturbance was resolved.

"So how do you know her?" Bell asked as they strolled back to the car.

Riley turned to him, her eyebrows raised. "You really want to know?"

"I'm curious. Cone of silence between partners, I swear."

Riley sighed. They arrived at the car, and she put her hand on the roof, considering how much to tell him. "We dated in college."

"Ah." Bell's eyes widened ever so slightly, though Riley dating women was one of the worst kept secrets in the station. "And was she in the same line of work?"

Riley laughed. "Not at all. She studied dance and literature, wanted to be a prima ballerina and write the next great American novel.

"She hit a rough patch after we broke up. I was in the academy and she wouldn't speak to me, but I heard through mutual friends she had fallen a long way from her aspirations."

"Why? What happened?"

"It's not my story to tell. Suffice it to say, I'm not surprised things went the way they did. I feel for her. When I run into her, every so often, I try to be kind. She's not a bad person."

Chapter 4

The rest of the shift was uneventful, a couple of calls to deal with drunken mischief, but overall, a breeze for a Friday night.

Bell was a good rookie, asked intelligent questions, didn't leap to conclusions, or run toward danger. He didn't even get in the way most of the time. She told the Watch Commander as much at the end of her shift.

"You should think about retaking the TO exam," he said.

"Yeah. I'll think about it." There were always so many things she had to do that pushed study down the list of priorities. Then again, her career was important. The new recruits needed people training them who weren't old, straight, white guys.

As she rode home, she thought about Petra. It was probably too late to text, but she did anyway, sitting on her bike parked by the house.

> Did you see Mike earlier? What happened? Are you okay?

Riley put her phone back into her jacket and went inside. At almost one in the morning, she didn't expect anyone to be awake. She put her head into the living room, where her mother was in bed and appeared to be sleeping.

"G'night mom," Riley whispered, before retreating and quietly closing the door. She went into the kitchen and made herself some microwave mac and cheese. She always got hungry after a shift and tried to limit the amount of take-out she bought to save money. It was too late to cook, she was tired, and it would have woken her mom.

Standing at the kitchen counter, eating her mac and cheese from the paper container, a jiggle and creak alerted Riley that someone had opened the front door.

The footfalls clomped heavily over the wooden floors. Riley winced, hoping her mom would sleep through it. No doubt Maddy had come home from a night out, too drunk to remember to be quiet.

Right on cue, Maddy stomped into the kitchen, pausing at the door.

"It's you," Maddy said.

"Yeah. Just finished work."

"Microwave dinner again, I see." Maddy's nose scrunched in disgust, her words slurring together a little.

"You want some?"

"No way."

"What do you want then?"

"It's my kitchen too. I'm allowed to be in here." Maddy's voice rose in volume with each sentence.

"Keep your voice down."

"Why?"

"Mom's sleeping. It's the middle of the night."

"Don't you get sick of telling people what to do?"

"What?"

"You. You're a cop, you tell people what to do all day. Sit around passing judgment on people, racially profiling kids whose only crime is being born poor. You know," Maddy paused to take a few wobbly steps closer to Riley and the fridge, "I bet you've beaten up some motherfucker who just happened to be in your way. All you cops are the same."

"You're drunk. I'll leave you to it."

"Too scared to even have a conversation? You used to be a nice person. You used to care about people. You would never have hurt Petra like that if you weren't so fucking hung up on being right all the time."

"I don't want to have this conversation with you right now."

Maddy was blocking the doorway to exit the kitchen. Riley couldn't leave without pushing her sister aside, and the mood she was in, it would probably escalate. Riley knew how to incapacitate her sister, but it would only emphasize Maddy's point.

"I never understood why you wanted to be a cop. No one in our family has ever done it. Is it just a power trip?" Maddy said, her voice bordering on a shriek. There was no way their mother was still asleep.

"You need to lower your voice." Riley used all her willpower to keep her own voice steady and measured.

61

"Fuck you, little miss perfect. Always doing the right thing, telling everyone how to live their life. You're not my mom."

"No, I'm not." Riley sighed. "Mom can't take care of you, and you're clearly incapable, so someone has to look out for you. I never asked to be the head of this family, but Dad died, and then Mom had the stroke. What I wanted didn't come into it. You have no idea what I had to sacrifice to look after everyone."

"You? Sacrifice? You do whatever you want, you always have, and then you come up with some reason you *had* to. And now you're trying the poor me routine? You're so full of shit." The color drained from Maddy's face and she leaned over and vomited all over the linoleum floor. Bright blue liquid, probably from Blue Lagoons—her favorite.

"Christ, how did you get so wasted?"

"I was trying to stop thinking about you." Maddy stepped back, bumped into the kitchen door frame, and had to steady herself to keep from falling into the puddle of bright blue sick.

"Are you going to help clean this up?"

Maddy shook her head, leaned against the door frame and slowly sank onto the ground. "I'm just gonna close my eyes."

"Great." Riley grabbed the paper towels and cleaned up the mess as best she could. It would need to be mopped properly in the morning, but for now, Riley wanted to get out of her sister's presence.

Being drunk wasn't an excuse for being an asshole. Why should Riley try to take care of the family when all they did was throw it back in her face? She wanted to cry, but not here.

Riley went to check in on her mom again. "It's okay, Maddy had too much to drink. She's okay now," Georgina lay on her bed, clearly awake. "I'm sorry we woke you."

Georgina mumbled something indistinct. Riley went upstairs to her room in the attic, stripped off her uniform, showered, and went to bed. She was tired to her bones, her eyes felt like sandpaper, but she lay there, listening in the dark.

Maddy paced around her room. She hadn't taken her boots off, no doubt keeping their mom awake too.

Despite the strong temptation, going down there to tell her to stop being such a child wouldn't have helped. At some point she must have fallen asleep, waking a little after nine. She hadn't slept long enough to feel refreshed by a long shot, and despite staying in bed she didn't get back to sleep. She had another shift with the rookie today—afternoon shift again on a Saturday night, likely to be a messy one.

Riley looked at her phone. Petra had replied earlier that morning.

> Mike wouldn't see me, so I gave the ring to Cindy. She may as well have it now. I never want to hear from him again.

Though the words were simple, they lacked Petra's usual bubbliness.

*Are you doing okay? I'm here if you
wanna talk. I'm working later today.*

Riley didn't need Petra to reply, just wanted her to
know she had friend if she wanted one.

Usually, Maddy would have been her confidante, but
with the argument the other night, it seemed unlikely
Petra would want to talk to her either.

*I may as well get up, make sure there are no more
drunken spills I need to clean up.* Riley threw her legs
out from under the covers.

She tiptoed down the stairs—the only thing worse
than drunk Maddy was hungover Maddy. Georgina was
still in bed and needed help to get up.

"Morning. You doing okay?" Riley asked.

Georgina waggled her head in the way they
understood meant *yes*.

"Sorry about Maddy, she was super bombed when
she got home, and then I made the mistake of prodding
the bear."

Georgina exhaled in an exasperated way.

"I know, I know. I need to let her be. It's hard. She's
being such a royal pain in the ass lately." Riley bent
down to help her mother sit up, and wiped Georgina's
face and hands. "I'll get you something to eat, yeah?"

Georgina couldn't eat on her own, at least not very
well. Her limbs didn't do what they were supposed to,
and her facial paralysis made it difficult for her to chew
anything.

She lived off blended homemade soups and if Riley
was pressed for time, or they ran out, baby food. It

wasn't ideal, but Georgina made it clear she didn't want to go into a home. Not that they could afford it even if she wanted to.

Riley put on a pot of coffee to brew while she helped her mom eat and changed her continence underwear.

When she finished, she went back to the kitchen and poured her first coffee for the day. The old adage about cops and coffee was true in her case. Her blood may as well have been half coffee.

She sat at the battered kitchen table, with her coffee and her chocolate cereal, listening for her sister to come back down.

I wonder if she even remembers the fight.

Riley was a bundle of nervous energy after listening for Maddy to get up for the last half an hour, and decided to get some fresh air.

The worst thing she could do at the start of a Saturday night shift was be on edge. Riley's preferred method of self-regulation was intense work outs—lifting heavy weights or boxing and sparring—but to do something that taxing before a shift was a mistake. A bit of cardio would be a better plan.

Riley changed into her workout gear, tight shorts with loose joggers on top, a sports bra that held her modest chest almost flat, and a t-shirt with the arms cut off. With her short-cropped hair and boxy frame, she'd been told she looked like a man a number of times, as though it would make her change how she behaved or presented herself.

Riley was secure in her gender—she was a woman who liked women, and the fact that she was not especially curvy had never bothered her. It hadn't ever been a barrier to getting laid. It was when she spoke to her lovers about her job, or her family, that they usually withdrew.

Janice was different. Riley had been the one to pull away from that relationship. She dropped out of college when her father died suddenly—collateral damage from gang violence was the official line, but Riley had always thought it was a load of shit.

Her dad had been a lawyer, corporate stuff. Riley suspected he was the type who would help a company hide money in off-shore accounts, or manipulate laws to benefit the bottom line, and his bonuses. Knowing he was a serial philanderer only added to her suspicion that he was not a trustworthy person. She'd joined the police because it was a profession with a good career path that didn't need a college degree, and fulfilled her need to assert herself as law-abiding, morally upstanding, and just.

What a joke she thought being a cop would prove that. It was just as full of rule bending and nepotism as any other industry, and that's to say nothing of the institutional discrimination. Give someone power, and most of the time it would corrupt them.

Riley tightened the laces of her sneakers and shook out her arms. Being in her head like this wasn't like her—the last few days had really shaken her up.

"Running off then?" Maddy said from the kitchen as Riley stepped off the stairs on her way out.

"I'm going for a run, yes."

"Geez, you're a sourpuss today."

"I wonder why." Riley didn't want to get into this same argument again.

"Just because I don't think Mike's a bad guy doesn't mean we have to fight."

Riley frowned at her sister. "That's not why I'm angry."

"Why then? It's not *your* boyfriend."

"Petra is really hurt. I knew telling her would upset her, but she deserved to know. You didn't help, and as far as I know, haven't apologized for the way you behaved to her."

"Why would I apologize?"

"What you said diminished her. Excusing Mike's lies, his infidelity, the fact that you were lying on his behalf, that's a betrayal much deeper than his. You've known Petra since you were kids. She's more like your sister than your friend, and you think she should just accept being treated like that? What happened to you?"

Maddy rolled her eyes. "Typical. You think there's a right answer. That a person can get through life, and come out on top, without fucking people over. It's not possible."

"Does that mean you won't apologize to her?"

"I don't need to."

"Wow. You really don't know her." Riley pulled open the front door. *This was pointless*.

"And you do? Grow up. She's never going to love you back." Maddy stared hard at her, waiting for a comeback, but Riley turned away and jogged down the steps.

She ran up the hill, pushing her limbs to climb faster, Maddy's words echoing in her head in spite of the physical exertion.

She's never going to love you back. Riley loved Petra like a sister, and Petra felt the same. She loved all the Holmes family. But that wasn't what Maddy meant—she said it like it was romantic love. That Petra was the reason all Riley's lovers wouldn't stay. That she was unavailable, closed off, locked into an unrequited love with a woman who didn't see her like that. A straight woman.

How dumb could you be, falling in love with your sister's best friend. If it had been a movie, she would have said it was ridiculous and unrealistic, and yet here she was, literally running away from the truth.

Riley stopped at the top of the hill, looking down over San Destino, suddenly unable to breathe. What she really wanted, what she had wanted for years, in fact, was a woman who didn't love her back.

***

Petra had managed to fall asleep despite her brain whirling through every interaction she'd had with Mike over the years trying to find signs of when he'd changed.

When she read Riley's text asking how it went and if she was okay, she started to cry. Again. She'd cried a lot in the last day. For someone who was known for being cheerful and resilient, she was shocked she could cry so much. It felt as though she was releasing things that had been building up inside her for a long time.

Pillion for a Police Officer

Mike had wanted her to be his arm candy, his sounding board, his comfort after a long day of moving other people's money around. He never had time for her needs. She had asked him to come out to her parents' place for Thanksgiving once, early in their relationship, but he'd said *no*.

Grant and Mary lived in Seattle. They even agreed to pay for the plane tickets, but it made no difference. Petra's parents always invited him to visit when she went to see them, but he never went.

In over five years of dating, he'd never met them. Who knows what he was getting up to while she spent time with her family. She shook her head. Petra wanted to be comforted; she wanted her mom.

"Hey," Petra said down the phone when her mother picked up.

"Hi sweetheart. What's happening?" Mary's voice sounded breathy, as though she'd caught her in the middle of doing something difficult.

"Is now a good time? I can call back."

"Yes, yes. I'm just bringing groceries up from the car. I did a jazzercize class yesterday, so my legs are full of lactic acid and it's harder to move than it used to be. I suppose that's my own fault. I shouldn't exercise." Mary laughed, Petra didn't. "You okay, hun? You normally love my jokes."

"Mike has been cheating with Cindy, and god knows how many others." Petra was exhausted. The weight of grief for her failed relationship felt as though she couldn't breathe, though her eyes were dry this time.

"Oh," Mary said nothing else for a while, just breathed heavily into the phone. When she had gotten her breath back, she started again. "How did you find out?"

"Riley. She saw him with her."

"Right... What will you do now?"

"I broke up with him. Gave him the ring back."

"Good."

"What?"

"Good. I was always a bit miffed that he wouldn't come to see us. You know we don't like to travel, especially to San Destino, too many bad memories, but he didn't have an excuse. He didn't want to be outnumbered. Your father said I was being ridiculous, seeing red flags when there weren't any, but now I feel vindicated."

"Don't say that."

"Why not?"

"I loved him."

"I know you did." Mary sighed. "That's why I didn't say anything. I thought if my baby girl thinks he's a good man, maybe I'm wrong. How long has he been cheating, do you think?"

"I don't know." Petra chewed her right thumbnail for a moment. "Maybe the whole time. And you know the worst part?"

"There's a worse part?"

"Maddy knew."

"Well, fuck me sideways."

"Mom! You swore."

"I swear on occasion, when it's warranted, and that was definitely worth an f-bomb. I thought Maddy

Holmes was a good, decent girl. How do you know she knew?"

"I was at her place when Riley told the both of us. She said it was a man's nature to sleep around. Said her dad did it too."

"You're kidding? Poor Georgina. If he wasn't dead already, I would wish ill on Todd."

Petra inhaled sharply—it wasn't like her mother to be this hard.

"I'm sorry, I've had a bit of a week. My tolerance for people's nonsense is much lower than usual."

"What happened?"

"Oh, nothing of much importance, just reminded me of some old stuff I had hoped to forget."

Petra waited, knowing her mother's need to fill any silence.

"I got a letter about my high school reunion, thirty years, and… well, of course I can't go, but it got me to thinking about how we don't see you much, and it made me sad."

"I'm sorry, that does sound like a hard thing to deal with."

"It is. One day I'll tell you why we left, the real reason, and why we don't come to visit, but not today."

"What do you mean the real reason? You said you lost all your money in a bad investment and had to take jobs in Seattle because no one would hire you."

"That was part of the reason we relocated, but not the reason we can't visit. I'm sorry, honey, I can't give you any more details."

Petra didn't know what to say. Her parents had left in a swirl of unanswered questions, but she had always assumed they'd thought her too young to get caught up in the trauma of it all, to fully understand. "Why didn't you take me with you?"

"To Seattle? To live on a hobby farm with no money?"

"Yes. What if I'd wanted to come? You didn't even ask." Why hadn't she asked her parents in the years since they'd moved? It was as though they all silently agreed not to discuss it.

"I…your father and I thought you would do better in San Destino. Your friends were there, the Holmes', your grandmother. Just because we were forced to move away didn't mean we had to ruin your life too."

Petra said nothing.

"I infer from your silence that you don't agree."

"It's not that, Mom, it's just… I dunno. It was really hard being left behind. I thought I'd done something wrong."

"Honey, no." Mary sniffled down the phone line. "I wish we'd never started this conversation. I'm going to have to go now. Do you have a friend who'll take you out? Or whatever you want to do? I guess Maddy is in the doghouse for the foreseeable future."

"Very much. I'll sort something out. Don't worry about me."

"Thanks for calling. Talk soon." Mary hung up, apparently too upset by reopening old wounds to offer her any further support, though Petra didn't know why she was surprised. She had always been an absent parent, even when she lived in the same city.

Petra had a couple of yoga classes to teach that day. Saturday was her busiest day, which was unfortunate given her low energy levels. Maybe she should give the classes a bit more of a yin flavor to reflect that.

She put on her workout clothes, gathered her hair into a messy bun on top of her head, and left to grab a coffee on the way to the studio.

Yoga Solutions Studio was in the Sentinel building, a few blocks from her apartment, in Juniper Hollow, the opposite direction to the Holmes's place, though it didn't guarantee she wouldn't run into one of them.

Riley was probably working. She seemed to take all the shifts she could get to pay for her mother's home care.

Maddy had never been good at supporting her family. Maybe she'd misjudged her best friend the same way she'd been blind to how much of an asshole her fiancé had been. Ex-fiancé. It was as though she'd been looking at life through rose-colored classes for years, and had only now started seeing the real world.

Petra's favorite coffee place was already packed, with a few locals lingering on the pavement waiting for to-go orders.

"Hey Petra, how's things?" Martin, her favorite server, smiled.

"I've been better, to be honest." Petra handed him the expensive insulated travel mug Mike had bought her after she complained about the huge amount of waste produced by to-go coffee.

He had given her lots of nice presents over the years, usually to apologize for something, but she could still get use out of those things. The *things* hadn't betrayed her.

"What's up, girl?"

"Heartbreak. Nothing time and a good strong coffee won't fix."

"You got it. I'll yell when it's done. I hope you're not in too much of a hurry." He flicked his eyes over the people milling around and the full seats. She paid for her coffee, but it would be a little while before it would be ready.

Petra hummed to herself, unsure where the song had come from, but the chorus from a Dolly Parton song rattled around in her head. She didn't even like country music, but it was cheery.

Maybe her brain jukebox had picked an upbeat song to keep her moving until she could collapse in a heap at the end of the day.

"Grande for Petra," Martin yelled over the crowd. She took the coffee from the counter and headed to the studio. If she made it through the day without crying in front of her students, she would reward herself with a bottle of pinot gris and Thai take-out.

***

The half-full classes gave her a much needed reprieve since she didn't require as much energy to keep them going, but a disappointment because her pay would be reduced.

As a freelancer, she earned what was left over after the venue took out their fees, and the fewer people in the class the smaller her portion. She'd never been too hard up, her parents could loan her a little if things were too tight, but it embarrassed her when she could only afford dahl and rice to eat or had no cash for advertising her classes.

The route home from the studio went past a small bodega where she got two bottles of wine, one for tomorrow, and an extra-large block of chocolate. The Thai place delivered, so she called to order as she walked. They would arrive five or ten minutes after her if everything went her way, though waiting would be fine.

At home, she pulled off her workout gear and changed into her lounging sweatpants and a tank top. The warm spring day had left her apartment muggy. She opened the balcony doors to get some airflow before pouring herself a glass of wine.

Petra's tiny balcony had just enough room for one of those hanging chair hammocks, a gift to herself after Mike told her they were far too boho for her if she wanted to be taken seriously. Every time she thought of Mike, she came up with a new reason to dislike him.

How could I have been so blind?

Just as she settled herself in the hammock chair, her doorbell buzzed. Trotting inside, the delivery driver appeared on the screen, holding her dinner.

"Hi, I'll be right there."

Ten minutes later, she had settled back into her hammock with a big bowl of pad Thai and green curry balanced on her lap.

The sun set over the water, sparkling with orange and yellow, then later reds and purples. Petra ate all the food she ordered. She usually prided herself on sensible eating—whole foods with lots of vegies—but heartbreak was an acceptable exception.

When the sun had sunk below the horizon, she went inside and put a soppy movie on the TV while she drank more wine.

At some point, she fell asleep on the couch and woke at about two in the morning with furry teeth and a dry mouth. She got up long enough to struggle into the bedroom before falling asleep again.

Full light streaming in through the windows woke her. In her sleepy state, she'd never closed the blinds. Still fully clothed on top of the bedding, she regretted the choices from the night before.

There's a reason I don't drink that much. She held her hand to her forehead in the vain hope it would help.

In the kitchen she found both bottles of wine in the sink, one empty, the other half full. No wonder she felt terrible. It was well after eleven, and though her stomach was empty, the thought of eating made her feel nauseated.

She found her phone lodged down the side of the couch after five minutes of searching. There were no notifications. The last message came from Riley yesterday, saying she was there if needed.

Pillion for a Police Officer

Petra had a small social circle—she was picky about her friends—but with Mike's connections, she had been invited to more parties and lunches and dinners than she had wanted to attend. Now they were over, her friends predominantly consisted of the Holmes sisters, and she wasn't speaking to one of them. She texted Riley.

> Are you up for a chat today? I'm feeling
> a bit sorry for myself.

With Riley's work schedule, there was a good chance she would be busy, or else exhausted, but it was worth asking. Petra cleaned her teeth and tipped the remaining wine down the sink lest she be tempted by it later on. Her phone buzzed not long after.

> Wanna have dinner? I could bring take-
> out to your place if you want?

Petra smiled. Riley was so sweet. She'd been steadfast in her support through Petra's life, especially after her parents had moved away.

It was as though Petra hadn't thought of her as her own person, more of an extension of Maddy, but through the lens of the last few days, she started to realize the eldest Holmes sister was the best of them.

She'd given up college to come back to San Destino and take care of them after their dad died, and then when Georgina had her first stroke, she'd become the caretaker of the family. In many ways, Petra had taken her for granted the way Maddy and Jen had. None of them had given her the credit she deserved.

Pull yourself together. Take care of Riley for once. She always takes care of everyone else.

> How about I cook? I bet no one has cooked for you in a long time. Plus, it'll give me something to do with my afternoon. Say six o'clock?

She smiled as she sent the reply. Home cooked meals were comforting, and this would allow her to do something nice for a friend who had been there, quietly supporting her without ever asking for anything in return. But what should she make?

Riley was a straightforward eater, meat and potatoes, meat and salad, mac and cheese. Sometimes she'd go as far as a lasagna but that got toward the fancy end of her spectrum.

The Holmes family rarely ate out, and when they did, they chose Chinese egg rolls, fried rice, kung pao chicken.

Petra was more adventurous, often cooking vegetarian curry dishes, and ayurvedic foods preferred by the yoga schools she'd studied at.

Something in between would be best, and nothing with tofu. Riley hated tofu. The family all teased her about it, though most of her police buddies agreed.

A Japanese style curry, with beef and sticky rice came to mind. Petra had bookmarked the recipe online weeks ago, but hadn't had the opportunity to try it out yet.

She had most of the ingredients in the house, though she needed to buy some beef. With a mission and a deadline, Petra showered, vacuumed her small apartment, cleaned the kitchen ready for cooking, and headed down to the butcher.

Having something to look forward to lifted Petra's mood, and she even caught herself humming a song she'd heard somewhere but didn't know the words to. She wasn't much into music. She had her yoga class soundtracks, with a lot of pan flutes and steel drums, but the rest of the time she let the radio or streaming service choose for her.

Riley had played in bands in her youth, as the drummer. She'd snuck Petra and Maddy into gigs, but after Riley joined the police, she'd given that up too. Petra couldn't believe she hadn't seen how much Riley had sacrificed.

Too caught up in my own shit to see it, and maybe too much listening to Maddy.

Back at home she chopped the vegetables. Petra's clairvoyance, or whatever helped her with the hospice patients must be faulty, or else it required her to direct it.

Now she refocused it to her best friend's sister and saw all the pain, denial, and self-sacrifice she should have seen years ago.

She'd inadvertently shut off her inner feelings to avoid being hurt by Mike, and it had spilled across everyone else.

A wave of emotions moved through her body—grief, loss, sadness, unrequited love, reined in anger, disappointment—and she reeled back from the kitchen bench, almost dropping the knife. As she came back to herself, the doorbell buzzed.

Riley.

"Hey, come up," she said into the intercom. All that afternoon, thinking about Riley seemed to have connected them in a way she'd never experienced before. But she must have that wrong. Riley was happily single, or so she said.

As a gay woman in the police force, Petra always assumed she'd chosen not to be in a relationship to avoid the worst of the homophobia. But that fleeting, intense connection to Riley's center showed it was more than that—she loved someone who didn't know she existed.

Petra opened her apartment door just in time for Riley to round the last of the stairs. She smiled and waited. Riley's walk had a little more spring in it when they locked eyes.

It's me. She loves me. It suddenly made sense how defensive she'd been about Mike, and how upset she was with Maddy. *How could I have been so ignorant?*

"Thanks for inviting me over," Riley said, leaning in for a hug. Her strong arms had Petra's heart beating a little faster, and her breathing fast and shallow. Was she lingering too long?

"Come in." Petra smiled. "I haven't got as far as I would have liked with dinner. Sorry about that." She waved her arm over the kitchen counter, still covered in ingredients for the curry.

"That's alright. I'm not in a hurry." Riley stood awkwardly near the dining table.

"Can I get you a drink?"

"Can I give you a hand?" Riley said at the same time. They both laughed. Petra's face heated giddy as a schoolgirl. This had never happened before, not even with Mike. But then again, she shouldn't use him as a guide for romance.

"No, just chill out. You can talk to me while I chop. The kitchen is too small for two, anyway."

Riley sat at the table. "I'll have a coffee if you're making something, otherwise water is fine."

"Coffee coming right up." Petra busied her hands with the coffee maker before turning back to the cooking. "Tell me about your day?"

Riley smiled wearily. "Last night was hectic. I got given a rookie to look after while a couple of the other TOs were off sick or busy with other assignments. It's been interesting trying to get him to act like a cop, but he seems like a good kid."

"I'm sure you're a great trainer." *You spend so much time coaching your sisters, and me, you're a pro already.*

"That's sweet of you to say."

"Here's your coffee." Petra handed over the mug, straight up and strong just like Riley.

Her fingertips brushed over Riley's and a little thrill ran up her arm, down her spine, and settled in her groin. That had never happened with anyone, ever. Petra swallowed hard and turned to throw some onions into the pan.

81

Chapter 5

The coffee was strong, with a hint of berry and chocolate, much nicer than the stuff Riley bought for herself, or the swill they passed off as coffee in the station.

Petra kept chatting, sounding chirpy, even happy, which seemed strange given the breakup had happened so recently.

Don't ask too many questions, you don't want to jinx it. The food smelled so good. Petra was an excellent cook, and seemed to enjoy the process as much as anything else.

Riley reluctantly made meals, preferring to repeat the same foods over and over, classics that she'd perfected. The idea of trying a new recipe added unneeded stress. With all the drama and pressure of her job, food needed to be comforting and straight forward.

Whenever Petra turned to the stove, Riley's eyes were drawn to the shallow V-shape of the apron strings around her waist, the dangling bow that swished over her gorgeously proportioned bottom.

Stop ogling her, get it together. Not the time, not to mention Petra was straight.

At that moment, she realized Petra was asking her something. "Sorry, what?"

"Will you go for your TO exam again?" Petra turned her head, their eyes locking.

"Yeah, the Watch Commander thinks I should, and I've had a nice enough time with this rookie. I don't want the newbies all trained by the grumpy, straight, white men in the department. Gotta give the grumpy lesbians a turn sometimes."

Petra giggled, her laugh bubbling up and spilling out, making the room feel somehow lighter, warmer. The dull ache in Riley's chest deepened.

"I think you're a great teacher. You've had to take on so much with your mom and sisters. I really admire you. I don't think I've ever said that."

Riley scoffed, nearly spitting out her coffee. "Thanks, but I'm a hot mess. It's a miracle anyone in the family still speaks to me."

"Surely they know you're the glue holding everything together nowadays."

"Some glue."

"What do you mean?"

"Maddy and I are...not really on speaking terms just now."

"Oh." Petra stirred the curry.

"Yeah. I don't know what to do about it. I tried to tell her she was out of line the other night, with you, but she thinks I was out of line." She hesitated. "I feel like she's not who I thought she was."

"I've had a few revelations over the last few hours too…"

"What? You can tell me anything, you know."

"I know I've spoken to you a little about the feelings I get."

"Yeah."

"I probably never told you how much I can actually feel. I thought I knew Mike, and you, and Maddy, but today I turned the switch back on."

"And?" Riley prompted after a long pause.

"I'm sorry I never noticed you for you."

"What do you mean?"

"All the stuff you do for your family. For me. I never appreciated how much it cost you."

Time slowed down. What did she mean? It hadn't cost her that much. Sure, she'd had to pivot her career, and she lived with her mother, and she hadn't had a relationship for years, and she kept missing out on promotions because she had to deal with crises with her mother and sisters.

"You're doing so much. And without complaint."

"There are some complaints." Riley tried to smile. Her chest felt tight, as though she couldn't quite get enough breath.

"You're allowed a few complaints." Petra's smile dazzled, her straight white teeth, a little bit of gum below the top lip, and the little wisps of bright red hair that curled around her hairline. If she hadn't been in love with her sister's best friend before tonight, she was in this moment. Riley glanced at her coffee cup, willing her cheeks to cool down.

As though Petra caught her awkwardness, she turned away and cleared her throat.

I've blown it now, made her uncomfortable mooning over her. She mentally kicked herself for being so unable to control her feelings. Feelings she'd managed to keep to herself for years, which now needed release, whether either of them liked it.

They stayed silent for a while as Petra served their meal and put it out on the beautiful, pale wood dining table.

"I thought we could have iced tea with our food. I went a bit overboard with the wine last night." Petra looked down and away as she admitted the overindulgence.

"I'm happy with that." *No wine should help me keep my libido in check at least.*

"How's your mom been?"

"Y'know, much the same."

"I'll have to come around to talk with her."

"She would love that. It always sounds like you're having a full conversation, even though I can only hear your side. Like you're on the phone." Riley took a bite of the Japanese curry—velvety and smooth with a delightful umami flavor and a hint of heat. "This is amazing, really."

"You're just saying that, but you're welcome." Petra smiled and took a bite. "You know Georgina and I do have conversations. I can hear her side."

Riley hesitated, considering the statement. Petra had mentioned this ability of hers and Riley had always thought it was imagined, or possibly metaphorical, but if she really could talk to her mom, then maybe… "What does she say?"

"The usual stuff. She knows what's going on. You're her favorite, not that she would use that word, but she's been let down by Maddy's wild choices and Jen still acts like a child."

"She said that?"

"About Jen?"

"No, about me." Riley's cheeks heated again.

"She's very warm about you. Always saying how much you do for her, keeping everything running. For a while I thought she was being over the top, but I've realized today, she isn't. You keep the family together. Me included." Petra put her fork down and looked Riley straight in the eye. Her cheeks had turned the most delicious pink, her eyes wide and almost sparkling in the warm golden light.

If she didn't know any better, Riley would think she wanted to be kissed, but that was silly.

Petra took Riley's hand in hers. "You're amazing. I've only just seen it."

"Don't tease." Riley tried to pull her hand away. This couldn't be real. It must be some sort of horrible joke. Maybe Maddy had put her up to it as a prank, or revenge.

"I'm not teasing. You're strong, capable, caring. I've been so unaware about so many things—Mike, Maddy.

But I see in your heart Riley Holmes." She put her other hand on Riley's chest.

Hot, thudding, racing. Petra had to feel it all through her clothes.

Riley pushed her chair away and stood up. "This isn't funny."

Petra looked stunned, her forehead creased with confusion. "I'm not joking. I know you've loved me for a long time, and I... thought this was what you wanted?"

"I don't want to be a pity fuck. And you don't even like women."

"You're not my first. And I don't want you out of pity or obligation. I'm seeing you in a way I never had before—the fierce, protective, nurturing person I've been looking for all my life and you've been right under my nose."

Her head spun. Too much, too quick. Riley felt drunk, her arms and legs seemed to belong to someone else. "I need a minute," she said and strode toward the balcony. She sank into the hammock chair which bounced and rocked.

This couldn't be happening. Riley had fantasized about Petra for so long, she had wished for this moment, but now it felt wrong. She must be rebounding. She'd dumped Mike barely days before.

Maybe she was still drunk from last night. Then again, she didn't seem drunk—she seemed happier than she had been in months.

Petra had never been a prankster, and after the fight with Maddy, it seemed unlikely she'd do something like this even if she'd been asked to. One of the things Riley loved about her was her unwillingness to compromise, even for a close friend.

"Can I come out?" Petra stepped onto the balcony, two beers in her hands.

"Sure."

"Do you want one? I thought it might take the edge off. I know I said I wasn't going to drink, but that went so spectacularly badly, maybe I need one."

Riley laughed. "I would love a beer."

"I'm sorry."

"Don't be. I'm sorry I reacted so..."

They each sipped the beer, its cool herby flavor helping to bring Riley back to herself.

"The thing is, my psychic abilities, I've been suppressing them."

Riley stayed silent, waiting for her to elaborate.

"In my heart, I knew there was something wrong between Mike and I, so I stopped listening to the messages around him, and around my friends. It gets too painful to hear what people really feel and think when they're close to you.

"With the people in the home, they're on their way out of this life. They want comfort, they deserve companionship, so I turn it on for them. I listen with all my being, and I help them cross over when it's time."

"Okay." Riley had never heard her speak this candidly about her ability.

"I woke up this morning miserable, so I opened myself up. I looked into Mike's heart, and I saw how vain and shallow he is. I looked at Maddy, and she was…well you know how she is. She doesn't really think about other people much. Then when I felt really alone, I felt you. The person who has been looking out for me, caring for me, and I saw how you felt."

"Oh."

"You've hidden it so well. You never made me feel uncomfortable."

"I thought you were straight."

"There are things I haven't told you, or Maddy. She's not what you would call discreet."

Riley laughed again, releasing a weight from her chest. "No."

"If you don't want to, y'know, I totally understand. I sprung it on you unexpectedly but, you're worthy of love, just the way you are."

"Come on now."

"I'm serious," Petra said, stepping forward. She stood only inches away, and the smell of her coconut shampoo caught in Riley's nostrils. She looked away, but Petra reached out and turned her chin back toward her. "You're beautiful."

Was this real? It would be easy to give in to this invitation, to leap up and kiss Petra long and hard, as she'd wanted to do for so long, but was it right? "What about Mike?"

"What about him?"

"Don't you want to, I dunno, wait a little while?"

"No. My mind is clear. I feel you. I want you."

Riley had never had someone declare themselves so openly. It was equal parts refreshing and terrifying. "I'm—it's all very sudden."

Petra took Riley's hand. "Come back inside. We'll eat dinner and maybe watch a movie. There's no rush."

Without words, Riley followed her back into the apartment, and they sat down. The food had gotten a little cold, but that was okay.

She kept smiling, like a giddy school girl. Petra knew how she felt, and she felt the same. Maybe it wouldn't last, but Riley wasn't willing to turn down the opportunity.

As they sat at opposite ends of the couch, watching a nineties Sandra Bullock rom com, Riley wanted more than anything to curl up with her, but it felt rushed. She worried the dream would shatter if she pushed too hard.

The end of the film, where the two main characters fell into one another's arms, embraced, and laughed— fuck, she yearned for that feeling. She turned and caught Petra looking at her.

"Sorry," Petra said, turning back to the screen.

"What for?"

"I was staring."

"Yeah, you were." Riley smiled.

"I was thinking about what it would feel like to kiss you."

Riley didn't know what to say. Her mouth was dry and her palms were damp—she'd been thinking about it too.

"I think you should kiss me."

Pillion for a Police Officer

Riley took a breath and moved up the couch, the credits of the film rolling, but she didn't pay any attention.

Petra leaned in, her lips so close, her feathery breath grazed Riley's skin, and the next moment she'd closed the distance.

Petra's lips met hers—full, moist, warm, and giving, just as she'd hoped they would be, just as she'd imagined. They tasted of beer, and the subtle undercurrent of Petra's natural flavor.

Riley's neck and cheeks became hot, and her groin tingled. She put her hand up to Petra's face, sliding her fingers back into her fiery red hair, grabbing it to pull her closer, deeper.

Petra moaned and leaned further into the kiss. Riley pulled her back until she almost lay on top of her. Riley's fantasies paled in comparison. The real thing, the real Petra, the pressure of that sweet, silky body right there in her arms was better than any other experience she'd ever had.

Riley snaked her other arm around Petra's body to pull her closer, palm to the small of her back, pushing down.

She pulled away, and Riley went to protest, until she repositioned herself straddling her. The warmth of her thighs, and what lay between, burned into Riley's pelvis. She wanted so badly to rip their clothes off and take her right there, but this wasn't a sprint. It needed to be sweet and delicate, strong and rough, but never fast.

Petra's hands roamed all over her body, sometimes feathery, sometimes clawing. She unbuttoned Riley's shirt, and threw it open, pulling off her own sporty tank top, revealing her alabaster skin and tiny pink nipples. She wasn't wearing a bra, not that she needed to with her perfect, upturned breasts.

"Oh god," Riley moaned. Petra leaned forward and Riley's mouth found one of the nipples. She arched her back in response, her nipple hardening further into a rosebud of excitement under Riley's lips and tongue. Her hands moved around Petra's back and over her bottom, all the yoga she did giving her excellent definition and flexibility.

Riley had wanted to do this for so long, making it hard to keep her mind in the moment, but she wanted to savor it, in case this was a one-time-only thing.

She moved her mouth to the other nipple, this one already hard, and Petra's breath caught erratically in response.

"Mmm…" she mumbled.

Riley kept her tongue and lips pressed to the delicate, fragrant skin. As she did so, her hand swept its way down Petra's belly, which trembled a little as she moved over it, and stopped at the waistband of her sweatpants.

Petra's hips tilted, as though urging Riley to move lower, and when Riley hesitated, she shuffled closer, opening her knees to allow her in.

More than anything, she wanted to strip Petra naked, pull her onto her lap, get skin to skin, as though trying to meld their bodies together. But the anticipation was so good.

Petra reached down to pull Riley's face back to hers and kissed her deeply. Riley ran her hand under Petra's leg, pulling it up.

Petra broke the kiss and moved so she straddled Riley again, the heat from her groin like fire. Riley exhaled, trying to keep herself calm, but it wasn't working. The urge to pick Petra up, carry her to the bedroom and ravage her until they couldn't move was overwhelming.

Petra ground her pelvis onto her lap, kissing Riley's neck and ears. Riley's hands slid over her hips, butt, and thighs. Petra moaned and pushed herself forward, but Riley held back.

"Should we take this to the bedroom?" Petra said, breathless.

"We could... or we could stay here?"

"Are you teasing me?"

"A little." Riley grinned and looked into Petra's flushed face.

"If we stay on this couch, will you fuck me?"

"Yes, eventually."

Petra moaned, a frustrated but aroused sound. "You're killing me."

"We only have the first time once; I don't want to rush anything."

Petra pushed her hand down between Riley's legs, making her gasp. Riley grabbed her wrist, grinding herself onto Petra's hand, sure that her wetness had soaked through her jeans.

"When you put it like that, how can I refuse?" Riley said, sliding her other hand into the front of Petra's pants.

***

After they were both spent, having explored one another's bodies, bringing each other to the point of climax several times, the two women were sprawled together on Petra's living room floor, sweaty, sleepy, and satisfied.

"Wow," Petra said.

"Yeah."

"I—"

Riley turned to her. "What?"

"Your stamina is—let's just say I had more orgasms with you just now than in the last six months with Mike."

Riley laughed. "You're joking? What was he doing?"

Petra looked away. "I've come to realize he is only interested in himself. Whenever I orgasmed with him, it was an accident."

"I'm so sorry." Riley ran her hand down Petra's cheek. "So, did you enjoy that?"

"Definitely. Five stars."

They both laughed. It was a relief to know that Petra had had a great experience, although, given what she'd said earlier about other things she hadn't shared with Maddy, Riley was curious how much experience she'd had with women.

Time had gotten away from her; it was after midnight. She wanted to stay curled up beside her love forever, but the carpet under her started to itch, and the cooling sweat from their activities raised gooseflesh along her arms.

"Are you cold?" Petra asked.

"A little."

"Should we shower before going to bed?"

"Are you cool with me staying?"

Petra frowned. "Do you not want to? Do you need to go home for your mom?"

"Of course, I want to. I just… didn't want to make assumptions."

"You're so used to people treating you like shit. After what we just did, sharing my bed would be the perfect end to an amazing night."

"Are you sure?"

Petra sighed and looked away, her hand roaming along Riley's arm as though without intention. "Mike didn't like sleepovers. He stayed here a few times at the start, but then if I wanted to sleep with him, it had to be at his place, and it was only a couple of times a month."

"And that didn't seem like a red flag?" Riley frowned.

"He had excuses. He had to get up early, or needed to work on stuff I wasn't allowed to see, but yeah, in hindsight, I should have known earlier he was up to something."

"Don't beat yourself up. You're such a positive person—you want to see the best in people. You didn't do anything to deserve that." Riley kissed Petra's forehead. "Shall we get some sleep?"

Petra nodded.

***

They spent the night curled against one another. Riley's smooth, muscular form felt both strange and familiar at once. Mike never liked to cuddle even when he did stick around after sex.

In only a few days it had become clear that her relationship had been a sham; someone for him to parade in front of his work colleagues, or parents. Even when they were engaged, he hadn't changed his behavior, always ready to leave. Had he been treating her like an accessory on purpose? Or was it that she was so agreeable it left her needs unmet?

And now she had fallen straight into bed with someone else which was on the top of the list of things not to do after a breakup. Maybe it was okay, given she had known Riley for a long time, they were good friends, and her feelings weren't new.

"Morning," Riley murmured into her back. "How did you sleep?"

"For someone who isn't used to sharing the bed, I was surprised how good it was."

"Like we're meant to be together?"

Petra stiffened. Only days ago, she'd thought she and Mike that were meant to be together, but that had been built on a sea of lies she had missed. This was too soon, she'd made a mistake, no matter how good the sex was.

"What just happened?"

"Nothing." She pulled away and went to the bathroom. When she came back into the bedroom, Riley had disappeared. Petra walked into the kitchen and Riley was pulling her shoes on.

"I'll go."

"You don't have to go."

"I think I need to give you some space."

"Will you stop running away for one minute?" Petra put her hand over Riley's on the kitchen counter. "I don't regret what we did. I was... worried about the timing. Maybe we need to wait."

"Why?" Riley's foot was poised with her left shoe half on and half off.

"I've just come out of a long-term relationship. I don't want this to be a rebound fling."

Riley smiled and exhaled deeply. "Is that all?"

"Is that all?" she echoed.

"I thought you hated me or something, which would suck, but I can work with this." Riley smiled. "I'll wait for you until you're ready to explore this properly, but I don't think you need to worry. Not all rebounds are bad. Not all break-ups leave a person scarred."

Petra frowned. Maybe she was right? It had felt so good. So right with Riley in her arms, and in her bed. "Let me meditate on it, and then I'll feel better about moving forward."

"You know where I live. But I do have to go now. Maddy says I need to get home—I wasn't running away. I'll talk to you soon."

Neither of them spoke for a brief moment as though not knowing whether to hug, or kiss goodbye. In the end,

Riley leaned forward to kiss her, a chaste peck on the lips.

After the door swung closed behind her, the silence in Petra's apartment felt oppressive. It was as though her joy had left with Riley. Without her, things felt darker, less vibrant. She sighed.

I said I was going to meditate on it, and I guess that's what I need to do.

***

Riley got home to find Georgina alone. Maddy had said she would wait for Riley or the home care nurse to come, but hadn't.

"Hey Mom, you here on your own again?"

Georgina mumbled something unintelligible that Riley took as agreement.

"I'm sorry I wasn't here last night. I…" she hesitated, was this something she should share? What harm could it do? "I spent the night with Petra."

Georgina burbled excitedly.

"Calm down, it's not that big a deal." She wiped a little trail of drool from her mother's face and sat down on the couch not far from her mother's favorite chair. "Alright, maybe it is a big deal. I've had a crush on her for a long time, you knew even before I did. Last night I had intended to go around as a friend, after the blowup with Maddy, and her and Mike breaking up—"

Georgina squeaked.

"Sorry, did I leave that bit out? Petra dumped his ass. After seeing him in the car with Cindy, some woman from his office, Petra went up there and told him where he could stick his ring. So, I went round to comfort her but in the end she… we… well, I didn't think she liked women, but I was wrong."

Georgina seemed to take that as good news, jerking her head around with a vigorous nod.

"This morning, she… said she needed time to get over the breakup. She could have just been saying that, being kind, but I think she really meant it. I guess I bide my time a little longer, until she's sure it's not a rebound thing."

Georgina's hand twitched.

"Yes, I know it's only been a couple of days. I'm not blaming her for wanting to take some time. It's been years already, a few weeks, or months even, isn't going to change how I feel. And now I know she might feel the same, it's like—" she stopped for a moment, getting all her thoughts in order.

"It's like I've been asleep and now I'm awake. Everything I was doing before was going through the motions—work, friends, looking after you, Maddy, Jen. But now, I guess all the songs make sense. Isn't that what you said love was like?" Riley turned to her mom, whose eyes welled with tears. "It's okay, Mom, I'm alright. I'm amazing actually."

Her mind went back to the feeling of Petra's silky-smooth skin against hers. She'd held her all night. And in the morning, though she had been a bit strange, Riley couldn't fault her. This time last week she'd had a fiancé and her life all worked out. Now that had all changed.

"I'll make you a coffee. Have you eaten breakfast?" Riley said, her own stomach grumbling in response.

Georgina wobbled her head indicating *no*.

"I'll be right back."

Riley put on some blues music, something to keep her and her mother company while she was in the kitchen.

Despite how Petra had responded this morning, Riley couldn't help grinning. The thing she'd dreamed of for years had finally happened. Hope for a relationship—something there hadn't been before last night—had become a possibility even if she had to wait.

She made a fresh pot of coffee and waffles, though she had to look in the very back of the cupboard to find the machine.

Waffles were one of Georgina's specialty breakfast foods. She would make chicken and waffles, or bacon and waffles, but they didn't have any of either in the fridge. Riley made a mental note to go to the store for some later.

"Here we are," Riley said when she brought the feast into the lounge where her mother was sitting with her eyes closed. "I got a bit enthusiastic, and there's a hell of a mess in the kitchen, but that's for later." She laughed, still feeling quite giddy.

Georgina's eyes widened in surprise at the spread.

"I know you're not really supposed to eat all this sugar, but I thought for a little treat you could try some. If you don't want it, I can get your bran cereal instead, and I'll have your share."

Riley had finished her plate of waffles and her coffee, while Georgina had managed to get through almost half a waffle, which was quite good for her, before the home care nurse arrived.

Since her mom had become largely immobile, she didn't eat much. The nurse used the key safe to let herself in, as all three daughters had usually left the house when she came to care for Georgina.

At least Maddy paid her share of the healthcare bills. Riley remembered how often she would shirk her share of the caring duties. Jen was a bit flakey but would usually do her part when she wasn't out having drinks with her work friends, or on dates with men she met online.

As Georgina and the nurse went through her morning routine, washing her and then taking her through some physical therapy, Riley returned to the catastrophe she'd left in the kitchen, but even the trail of dirty utensils and flour spilled across the counter couldn't dampen her smile.

Petra liked her, and that was all she needed to know.

Chapter 6

Petra spent her day trying to calm the emotional turmoil inside her. Her body was all out of sorts with her head. She'd get a whiff of Riley's scent on the sheets and her whole body tingled, remembering the way she had touched her last night. Then, in almost the same moment, she would see the photos of her and Mike on the wall.

She looked happy, him with his photo face on—the stern jaw clenching look he thought made him look handsome but mostly made him look constipated.

I need to cleanse my space. She went through the apartment and found all the pictures of her and Mike, the gifts he'd given her that she'd kept, not because she liked them, but because she thought she had to. She brought them together on the dining table and looked at them.

What a meager pile to represent a relationship that lasted years. Though it was indicative of the way he thought of her—the gifts generic, and unsuited to her style, and the photos were always at events for his friends, or work colleagues.

Pillion for a Police Officer

She took the photos out of the frames and found an empty box that fit them all and put it by the door. The photos she put into the bottom drawer in her kitchen, telling herself she would deal with them later.

Petra had a bundle of sage she had used to cleanse the space when she moved in, along with some Tibetan singing bowls. She burned the sage, wafting the strong-smelling smoke over the apartment, especially around the doorways, and the bedroom, where Mike spent most of his time.

Sage cleared residual, unwanted energy. She would cleanse when she moved into a place, or started working in a new yoga studio, so she could start fresh, but this time she wanted to get Mike out of her head as much as out of her mind. Hopefully, it would help her powers work more reliably too, after masking them for so long.

When that was done, she used the singing bowls to create a sound bath in the living room. Then she was ready to meditate.

She sat on her yoga mat in the space in her living room she used specifically for mediation. It smelled nice, she had a soothing soundtrack of steel drum and pan pipes over running water, and she was comfortable in her lotus position, but her concentration wandered.

Inhale, hold, exhale, hold, she told herself over and over, but her mind's eye kept wandering back to Riley.

I don't want to rush into anything. I could really hurt someone I care for deeply by going into this half-baked. It's better to wait and let the emotional toll of Mike's bullshit settle a bit.

It sounded reasonable when Petra told herself to wait. That she was risking a great friendship, was being reckless, but her body still thrummed with Riley's energy.

Petra had never been touched like that, had never experienced that kind of attentiveness, that depth of pleasure before. Maybe it was a one off, but what if it wasn't?

What if the sex partners she'd had up until this point had all been garbage, and what she yearned for, without knowing, were Riley's skilled and patient hands and mouth. So many thoughts were whirling around in her head. So much had changed in the last few days, but it felt right. Despite the chaos it created, dumping Mike had been a relief.

Instead of calming her, the so-called meditation session excited her. She felt like a teenager, unable to think about anything but how long it would be till she could kiss Riley again.

Ridiculous. After twenty minutes of trying to achieve calm, Petra gave up. She dressed in her exercise gear and went out for a long walk. Perhaps she could achieve walking mindfulness instead.

Petra made her way through the streets taking in the houses, enjoying a glorious day. She walked through the billionaire's district, past the Sentinel building, the houseboats on Kismet Cove, before she found herself among the gorgeous terraced houses where the Holmes lived.

Pillion for a Police Officer

I didn't mean to go this way. She almost turned around. Instead, she closed her eyes briefly and used her gift to search for a reason she had been drawn here.

As though in the distance, she felt Georgina's presence, worried, but also excited.

Riley would be with her, Petra knew. But there was something urgent in the way Georgina's mind called out to her.

Petra made her way to the Holmes' house and knocked on the door. Riley answered and her face flowed through a range of emotions—delight, concern, before settling into a mostly neutral expression.

"Hey."

"Hey," Petra replied. "I've come to see your mom."

Riley frowned. "Okay." She stepped back and allowed Petra into the house. "I'm just cleaning up the kitchen. I'll leave you to it."

Petra couldn't miss the hurt in her eyes, but now wasn't the time to address it. "Thanks."

Georgina sat in her chair in the living room, listening to music, her face calm and a tiny smile on her lips.

"Hey Georgina. You wanted me to visit?" Petra said, sitting on the couch next to the older woman, and taking her hand so they could better communicate.

Yes. I wanted to talk to you. I didn't expect you to be here so soon. Riley told me about last night. Georgina's mind voice spoke clearly in Petra's head.

"I went for a walk. I've been trying to settle myself, but it's not working."

What do you want to settle?

"I just…" *I worry it's too fast.*

Do you know what I think?

Petra shook her head.

I think you're scared. Your man, Mike, who I never thought was worthy of you, by the way, has left your self-esteem shaken.

"No, that's not it."

Are you sure? I can feel all your nonsense about not wanting to hurt Riley, but she's tough. She knows what she's doing. She's been pining after you for years.

"That's exactly what I'm afraid of. She doesn't even know the real me."

And what real you would this be?

"The one who didn't see that her fiancé was a liar, who ignored all the signs, who hasn't made anything of herself."

Do you think you deserve to be punished because you fell for a man's promises? You're not the first extraordinary woman to be snared by one such as Mike, and you certainly won't be the last. But if you let that dictate your future, your happiness, then you really are a fool.

"Hey." Petra dropped Georgina's hand and sat back, stung by her words. One drawback of communication using her gift was that everything that was said came with all the emotions attached to it. Georgina was angry. Angry at her, but not for Mike.

You have to be ready for the lessons the universe needs to teach you. You weren't ready to learn the truth about Mike until now. But you have to lean into the discomfort of growth, of change.

"You've gotten very philosophical in your old age." Petra supposed being aware, stuck in a body that wouldn't do what you needed it to, would create a lot of time for thinking. She took Georgina's hand again and reconnected.

You are a beautiful soul. You deserve to be loved, adored, challenged. Riley is the one to do it, and all you have to do is turn to her.

"What if it doesn't work out?"

I don't think you have anything to worry about, but if it falls apart, you'll pick yourself up, and so will she, and in time you'll be healed. You don't get big love like this without risk.

She looked out the bay windows over the hilly street. Maybe Georgina was right—Mike had never been high risk. She knew he wouldn't challenge her. Maybe that's why she didn't look at his behavior too closely. But Riley had depth, she had courage, and ambition, and a kindness that scared her.

You can do this.

Petra pressed her lips together and nodded. "I can't get her out of my head. It's like I've never really seen her until now. And I can't turn these feelings off. I don't want to."

Georgina's lips trembled and jerked up at the left side into a smile. Her eyes were watery, and she looked like she was about to burst with emotion.

"Don't cry," Petra said, gently brushing a tear from her cheek.

Now, go and kiss my daughter.

Petra patted Georgina's hand, grateful to the woman who had been a better mother to her than her own blood.

***

"You off then?" Riley said, without turning around. She'd heard Petra's footsteps enter the kitchen.

"Not yet—what happened in here?"

Riley faced Petra.

"Did you use every dish in the house to make breakfast?"

"No, there are a few still clean." Riley couldn't help a small smile. *Dammit, I'm supposed to be giving her space, but she's not making it easy.*

"I'm sorry for… this morning."

Riley waited.

"I freaked out. It was too real. I've never felt like this about anyone before."

"And now?"

"Your mom and I had a chat. She thinks I'm a big idiot and sent me in here to make it up to you."

"Did she." Riley's half smile deepened. *That meddling old stick.*

Petra took two steps forward, hovering on the balls of her feet as though about to run away again. Maybe steeling herself.

Riley closed the gap between them and kissed her. Petra melted into her arms, and it was as though they would never be apart again. She felt so right.

"I'm so sorry," Petra said again, mumbling the words against her lips.

"Shh." Riley deepened the kiss. If she hadn't known better, she would have sworn she heard her mother cheering from the other room, but that couldn't be right. Riley stepped back and looked at the beauty before her. "I'm so glad you came back."

"Me too." Petra grinned and rested her head on Riley's shoulder.

THE END.

About the author

Fleur Blüm, a Melbourne-based writer, performer, and musician, crafts fiction with a romantic twist, infused with feminist themes. Balancing light and dark, she adds humor to narratives exploring tough topics.

Fleur has eight other published novels, and three poetry collections.

You can find out about Fleur, including book links and upcoming releases, at her website: www.fleurblum.com

www.ingramcontent.com/pod-product-compliance
Lightning Source LLC
Chambersburg PA
CBHW020532120726
47904CB00003B/1045